WITH TEETH

BRIAN KEENE

DEATH'S HEAD PRESS

Houston, Texas
www.DeathsHeadPress.com

Cover Art: Alex McVey

Book Layout: Lori Michelle
www.TheAuthorsAlley.com

BOOKS BY BRIAN KEENE

NON-SERIES
Alone
An Occurrence in Crazy Bear Valley
The Cage
Castaways
The Complex
The Damned Highway *(with Nick Mamatas)*
Darkness on the Edge of Town
Dead Sea
Dissonant Harmonies *(with Bev Vincent)*
Entombed
Ghoul
The Girl on the Glider
Jack's Magic Beans
Kill Whitey
Nemesai *(with John Urbancik)*
Pressure
School's Out
Scratch
Shades *(with Geoff Cooper)*
Silverwood: The Door *(with Richard Chizmar, Stephen Kozeniewski, Michelle Garza and Melissa Lason)*
Sixty-Five Stirrup Iron Road *(with Edward Lee, Jack Ketchum, J.F. Gonzalez, Bryan Smith, Wrath James White, Nate Southard, Ryan Harding, and Shane McKenzie)*
Take the Long Way Home
Tequila's Sunrise
Terminal
Thor: Metal Gods *(with Aaron Stewart-Ahn, Yoon Ha Lee and Jay Edidin)*
White Fire
With Teeth

THE LOST LEVEL SERIES
The Lost Level
Return to the Lost Level
Hole in the World
Beneath The Lost Level

THE LEVI STOLTZFUS SERIES
Dark Hollow
Ghost Walk
A Gathering of Crows
Last of the Albatwitches

THE EARTHWORM GODS SERIES
Earthworm Gods
Earthworm Gods II: Deluge
Earthworm Gods: Selected Scenes From the End of the World

THE RISING SERIES
The Rising
City of the Dead
The Rising: Selected Scenes From the End of the World
The Rising: Deliverance

THE LABYRINTH SERIES
The Seven
Submerged

THE CLICKERS SERIES *(with J.F. Gonzalez)*
Clickers II: The Next Wave
Clickers III: Dagon Rising
Clickers vs. Zombies
Clickers Forever

THE ROGAN SERIES *(with Steven L. Shrewsbury)*
King of the Bastards
Throne of the Bastards
Curse of the Bastards

THE GOTHIC SERIES
Urban Gothic
Suburban Gothic *(with Bryan Smith)*

COLLECTIONS
Blood on the Page: The Complete Short Fiction Vol 1
All Dark, All the Time: The Complete Short Fiction, Vol. 2
Love Letters From A Nihilist: The Complete Short Fiction, Vol 3
Where We Live and Die
No Rest For The Wicked
No Rest At All
Fear of Gravity
Unhappy Endings
A Little Silver Book of Streetwise Stories
A Conspiracy of One
The Cruelty of Autumn

Good Things For Bad People
A Little Sorrowed Talk
Stories For the Next Pandemic

NON-FICTION
End of the Road
The Triangle of Belief
Trigger Warnings
Unsafe Spaces
Other Words
Sundancing
Sympathy For the Devil: Best of Hail
  Saten Vol. 1
Running With the Devil: Best of Hail
  Saten Vol. 2
The New Fear: Best of Hail Saten
  Vol. 3
Leader of the Banned: Best of Hail
  Saten Vol. 4

MISCELLANY
A Field Guide To The Thirteen (*with
  Mark Sylva*)
Apocrypha
Liber Nigrum Scientia Secreta (*with
  J.F. Gonzalez*)

GRAPHIC NOVELS
The Last Zombie: Dead New World
The Last Zombie: Inferno
The Last Zombie: Neverland
The Last Zombie: Before the After
The Last Zombie: The End
Dead of Night: Devil-Slayer
He-Man and the Masters of the
  Universe: Origins of Eternia
A Very DC Halloween
DC House of Horror

This one is dedicated to Connor Rice . . .

ACKNOWLEDGEMENTS

My sincere thanks and appreciation to Jarod Barbee, Patrick C. Harrison III, and everyone else at Death's Head Press; Daniella Batsheva; Alex McVey; Matt Wildasin; Tod 'T.C.' Clark, Stephen 'Macker' McDornell, and Mark 'Dezm' Sylva; my grandfather Dee Keene (the G.O.A.T. of moonshiners); Keith Giffen (because I promised you a vampire novel); Mary SanGiovanni; and my sons.

ONE

HERE ARE THE things you need to know about vampires.

First of all, they don't dress in black. They're not high-cultured, well-mannered, nicely groomed or perfectly fucking coiffed. Vampires don't form secret societies and war with other creatures of the night. They don't hang out in cemeteries and tombs, listening to Bauhaus and Type O Negative and smoking clove cigarettes and whining about how much eternal life sucks. Vampires don't have existential crises, because vampires barely have any thoughts beyond what's for dinner. They don't feel love or angst. They're not romantic. Vampires are not sexy. They don't look like Bela Lugosi or Christopher Lee or Stephen Moyer. They don't behave like Dracula or Lestat or Edward Cullen.

Vampires do not fucking sparkle.

Forget everything you've seen in movies and on television and video games, and everything you've read in books and comics. The vast majority of that stuff is bullshit.

Vampires are more like sharks or rabid weasels than they are human beings.

Maybe you're laughing right now at the weasel comparison, but if so, then I reckon you've never seen what one weasel can do to a group of chickens. I see these hipster jackasses going on about free range chickens sometimes on social media, and I just shake my head, because it's clear to me that none of them have ever grown up on a farm or worked on one for any length of time. Free range farm animals end up as dinner for free range predators.

A few years back, a weasel got into my chicken house. That was despite me taking measures to proof the structure against predators. I had chicken wire encircling the entire thing—both the shack they roosted inside at night and the pen that served as their open-air enclosure during the day. I dug a good twelve inches into the dirt all around that chicken house, burying the wire fencing in the ground beneath it and then running it up overtop the pen and the shack. That thing was like Fort Knox. The chickens were protected from hawks and eagles up above, and foxes, rats and weasels from below.

Or so I thought.

One night, a weasel dug its way down underneath the pen, and then chewed through the wire itself, and managed to wriggle up inside the enclosure. The next morning, I was sitting out on the porch, drinking my coffee and scrolling through Facebook on my phone, and it occurred to me that I didn't hear the chickens. Usually, that time of morning, they'd be clucking and walking around, catching bugs and worms and basking in the early sunlight. Instead, there was just silence. I walked out to the pen and found out why. Every single one of my chickens had been slaughtered. The weasel had torn off each of their heads, one by one, and drank their blood. See, that's all a weasel cares about. He doesn't care about the meat or the fat or the innards. He just wants that warm blood. And when he'd had his fill of blood, the weasel left behind fourteen decapitated hens and two headless roosters. There were feathers strewn all about, but very little blood. The weasel had done a good job of getting all of that, like a drunk at the bar chugging beer directly from the tap.

And that's why I don't have chickens anymore, and why the coop is just sitting empty on my property with weeds growing inside of it and a roof that's starting to sag.

The chicken massacre traumatized my daughter, Alicia. I'd warned her again and again about getting attached to farm animals, but to be honest, I'd grown pretty attached to those chickens, too. It was probably a year before either one of us could eat chicken again, and in truth, she was able to do that long before I was. For a while, every time I tried to prepare chicken for lunch or dinner, all I saw were those headless bodies lying strewn about their pen, and yellow curds of fat bubbling out of bloodless, gaping neck stumps.

Alicia is supposed to go off to college this September. She wants to study Biometrics at West Virginia University up in Morgantown. Alicia is a lot smarter than I am. She gets that from her mother, Karen. She looks more and more like her with each passing year, too. Karen died of cancer when Alicia was twelve. We celebrated Christmas together in hospice that year, and she was gone before New Year's Eve. It's just been me and Alicia ever since, and I'm damn proud of her, even though I don't exactly understand what Biometrics is or what she wants to be when she graduates. She says that with Biometrics, she can get a job with the FBI, and looking back now, that's funny. Not funny in a Larry the Cable Guy stand-up comedy sort of way, but funny as in ironic.

You see, it almost came to pass that I would have paid for my daughter's college tuition by cooking meth.

But then the vampires happened, and in the space of one single night, everything changed.

Just like with the weasel.

Like I said before, just forget everything that you think you know about vampires. They aren't any of those things.

Particularly when they are hungry.

Hungry vampires are the worst of the bunch. They are vicious and mean. They're dirtier than pigs. They live and breed in filth, and they reek worse than roadkill. They're pale, hairless, scrawny fucking things, but also incredibly strong and unbelievably fast. It's been my experience that they don't go to art galleries or split the atom.

But that doesn't mean they aren't smart. On the contrary, vampires are wily and cunning.

Especially when they are hungry.

Ain't nothing more deadly than a hungry vampire.

Anyway . . . this happened just a few nights ago. Settle in for a spell and I'll tell you all about it.

TWO

THE REST OF the country likes to make fun of us here in West Virginia, calling us poor white trash or poor Appalachian trash or poor redneck trash.

Well, they're partly right.

We aren't trash. Say that around here and you're liable to get your ass kicked, and rightly so. But we are poor, for the most part, and we've been poor for generations. Mining and logging used to dominate the state, but environmental regulations and overseas efforts have gutted both of those industries. And even when mining was prominent, it was a dangerous job. A lot of workers got sick, injured or killed in the prime of their lives—decades before they would have reached the legal retirement age. If you think the big mining companies took care of their families, you'd better think again. Even with unionization, they found loopholes and ways around doing the right thing.

Farming was the state's other big industry, but I speak from some experience when I tell you that farming is a hard way to make a living—and these days, the living you make by farming ain't much of a living at all. I turned forty this year. I've been farming since I graduated high school. And each year, I've made a little less. The truth is, Karen's life insurance policy has paid the bills these last few years more than farming has. Were it not for that, I reckon my place would have been in foreclosure by now and Alicia and I would be homeless.

So, what else is there? Well, there's plenty of auto mechanics, but they ain't making much because everybody and their brother is also an auto mechanic. These days, folks can go on YouTube and watch a twenty-minute video about how to put a new transmission in their car, so there ain't much call for mechanics. Tourism has seen a rise in recent years, but there's only so many ski resort and mountain climbing and white-water rafting jobs to go around. There's service jobs—fast food restaurants and retail stores and the like—and while you can indeed earn a living wage working in such places, it's just that. A living wage. Just enough to get by, and no more. It's hard to build up any kind of savings for a rainy day when you're barely making over the minimum wage and limited to forty hours a week. And less than forty hours a week in many of those places, because if you're not working full-time, then they don't have to pay for your health insurance and other benefits.

Many folks in West Virginia rely on government assistance—welfare and other programs. Grow up with that, and you might tend to rely on it, too. And then your children will, as well. It's a vicious cycle, and it just breeds over and over again. Generation after generation of welfare recipients, never dreaming of reaching beyond that, simply because they don't know of any life beyond it. And even if you show it to them, it's hard to convince them to reach for it, when the safety of that government assistance is right there, warm and comfy like a security blanket.

And that's what it all comes down to, really. Security. Folks want the security of knowing that they won't starve or be homeless.

As a result of that, one of the main industries in West Virginia these days is meth.

People cook it, transport it, sell it, and use it. I read a news article that said the big drug cartels account for something like fifty percent of the methamphetamine in America, but the next biggest percentage is manufactured right here in West Virginia. And just like we do with everything else, we consume what we make. Rich folks have their cocaine and ecstasy and all those fancy designer drugs. People in West Virginia have meth.

And in a way, it's a family tradition, just like in that old Hank Williams Jr. song. After all, West Virginia was always known for bootlegging, back during the days of Prohibition. My great-granddaddy was a moonshiner—the biggest in Pocahontas County. He had a hollow deep out in the woods on the old home place, and that's where he cooked his shine. And he wasn't just making paint thinner. No, sir. This was decades before people started getting all worked up about organic food, but his moonshine was just that. He brewed different flavors—apple and raspberry and ginger, all from stuff that he grew himself or found growing wild out in the woods. It was high end, high octane stuff, and also high in demand. And not just from his neighbors. No, sir. Wealthier white folks from out of state paid top dollar for my grandaddy's stuff, and in a time of strict segregation, he was one of the few white bootleggers who would deliver to the black sections of the county. Indeed, he supposedly got a lot of shit from his fellow white folks for accommodating the black community, which only made him double down on doing it. When the heat got to be too much for him, he'd head across the border into Kentucky for a few months, and then come back to West Virginia once the law had moved on. Eventually, he reached the point where he was storing most of his moonshine in the basement of the county courthouse.

My cousins and I grew up hearing stories about great-grandaddy's bootlegging business. When he died, our grandparents supposedly destroyed the still and everything else, so that our parents—my dad and his two sisters—wouldn't get into it. The farm itself was handed on down through the family, eventually to my Aunt Lena, and then from her to my cousin, Terry.

A few years ago, Terry was in the process of tearing down one of great-grandaddy's old barns, so that he could use the space to grow pumpkins. The barn had been in sad shape back when we were kids, and time hadn't done it any favors. It was leaning horribly to one side, and the roof had all but caved in, and copperheads were breeding in the walls. Now, I don't like snakes so much, but copperheads always gave me a particular case of the willies. A rattlesnake will warn you before it bites. A copperhead gives you no such consideration. Copperheads are assholes.

During the demolition, Terry come across a sealed wooden box. Inside it were some old, yellowed composition notebooks, filled with great-grandaddy's sloppy scrawl. Terry was never great at reading or writing, so he brought them to me to decipher. It turned out that Terry had found our great-grandfather's handwritten moonshine recipes. The two of us, along with our other cousin, Gray, decided we'd try our hand at following in our kin's footsteps. We built a still in my garage. What we didn't realize was that making your own bootleg whiskey is an expensive hobby. And given that both moonshine and marijuana are both legalized now, that's exactly what it was—just a very expensive hobby. Eventually, we gave it up. I disassembled the still and packed it up, and it's still out there in my garage, just gathering dust. That was the end of our get rich quick scheme. Terry and I both kept farming, and Gray kept driving his dump truck.

What we didn't realize then was that a few years later, we'd circle back around to the idea of following in great-grandaddy's footsteps again. This time, not by distilling bootleg whiskey, but by cooking meth.

Except we never even got to that point, did we?

No, we never even made it past the hollow.

Hell, most of us never even made it out of that place.

Here's what happened.

THREE

HE WHOLE THING started when me, Terry, Gray and some of our friends were hanging out over at Terry's place one night, talking about our various money problems. With us were Donny Laudermilk, Darnell Witt, Mattie McMillion, and the Peters brothers—Cecil and Seymour. Yes, that's correct. His parents, who had about one brain cell between the pair of them, had seen fit to name one of their sons Seymour Peters. The other kids used to tease him mercilessly about it when we were younger. Hell, I guess we did too, some, and we were his friends. Things like "Hey, did you see more peters today, Seymour?" Or in middle school, when we all had to shower after gym class for the first time, "Hey, Seymour, I'll bet you'll see more peters now!" The teasing lasted until about eighth grade, when Seymour hit a growth spurt. That, combined with working on his daddy's dairy farm, seven days a week, turned Seymour into a hulk of a young man. The teasing stopped after that. He started playing football and made the wrestling team, and could have gotten a scholarship if he hadn't blown out his knee during his senior year. Instead, he'd graduated high school and gotten a job for one of the logging companies, and that had kept him in shape until two years ago when he got laid off. And as a result, Seymour had now started to get flabby, particularly around his midsection. But I still didn't mess with him.

His brother Cecil was the physical opposite—still as scrawny at age forty-one as he was at age sixteen. There was no sign of that middle-aged waistline bulge, and he didn't have a single gray or white hair in his beard. Of course, I'm being generous when I say beard. Cecil still had about the same amount of peach fuzz on his face that he'd had when we were in high school. The only place the years seemed to have impacted him was in the hair on his head, which had been steadily retreating since his early twenties. Because he still kept his hair long, years after the rest of us had cut ours short, he looked like a redneck Ben Franklin. As a result, Cecil never went anywhere without wearing a ballcap. These days, it was a bright red one with the former President's slogan scrawled across it. And when I say scrawled, I mean just that. Cecil hadn't been able to afford an official hat, so he'd made one himself—buying a generic red ballcap and writing the slogan across the front of the hat with a black magic marker. The campaign signs in his front yard during the election were of the same craftmanship. His shirt, however, although faded and starting to fray, wasn't homemade, and featured an unflattering slogan about liberals. Cecil had no subtlety. He wore his politics on his sleeve, quite literally.

Me? I didn't much care who was in office. Liberal or Conservative, they were all a bunch of crooks, far as I was concerned. They all promised change, but nothing ever seemed to change for us.

Cecil worked at the Walmart down in Lewisburg, as did Darnell. Like the Peters brothers, we'd all grown up with Darnell. And like Seymour, Darnell had gotten his fair share of teasing in school—not because of his name, but because of his color. Seldom was it anything outright racist. There were no crosses burned on his family's front yard, far as I know, and I only ever heard someone call him the n-word to his face one time. That was Matt Lewis, and Darnell beat that kid's ass so bad that Matt became something of a social pariah afterward, and Darnell became something of a begrudging hero. I reckon some of the others who used to hang around with Matt figured they'd better get on Darnell's good side, lest they get the shit kicked out of them, as well. Matt and his folks moved to Tennessee not long after. Darnell used to kid around and say it was because they were embarrassed that their son got beat up by a black man.

It wasn't until later in life, just over the last few years, in fact, that I came to realize that my perceptions of what Darnell dealt with when we were kids were probably very different than his recollections. Just because I didn't see a lot of overt racism doesn't mean he didn't experience it. Alicia told me that was White Privilege—a phrase which, until that moment, I'd always thought was kind of racist in and of itself. But when she explained it to me in that context, I understood better what it meant.

Neither Cecil nor Darnell were pulling down forty-hour shifts at Walmart. Cecil worked in the warehouse, and usually got a maximum of thirty-five hours per week—just enough that the store didn't have to cover his benefits. Darnell, who worked in the lawn and garden department, usually averaged twenty to twenty-five hours per week. Sometimes he got more than that in the spring, when his department was especially busy. Like myself, Terry, and Seymour, both of them were just squeaking by, financially.

The same could be said of Donny, but unlike us, he'd mostly made his peace with it. Donny had flunked out of high school our senior year, and was told he'd have to repeat the twelfth grade. For whatever reason, he'd never felt compelled to go back and revisit that final year, or earn his GED in the two decades that followed. He lived in a tin-roofed, three-room shack at the end of a dirt road up off Bald Knob (yeah, I know . . . we laugh at the name of that mountain, too). The place had running water and electricity, but just barely. He had no air conditioner, so it was sweltering inside during the summer, and on most nights, Donny would sleep in a hammock strung across his porch just to beat the heat. In the wintertime, he kept a woodstove burning all hours of the day, and while that made the place habitable, it was still drafty as all hell. Donny subsisted off his regular monthly welfare check, and whatever he could grow in his garden and shoot in the woods behind his house. He was a master when it came to different ways to cook a deer. Despite hunting all of my life, I only knew two ways to fix venison—fry some tenderloins in a skillet with a little flour and salt, or grind it up and put it in stew and chili. Donny was far more creative, and did all kinds of things with deer meat. And rabbit, bear, squirrel, wild turkey, and whatever else he could poach. I once told him he ought to get himself a YouTube channel and show folks how to cook wild game. Donny responded by asking me what YouTube was. He was the only one of us who wasn't on Facebook. In truth, I don't think he even had an email account.

You might wonder why nobody reported him for poaching all that wild game. After all, it's illegal to hunt deer and other animals out of season. Well, part of it is that nobody wanted to be a snitch. But mostly it's because a lot of other folks in these parts were in the same boat as Donny. People need to eat, and if you can't afford to drive down to the Walmart and buy some groceries, you make do with what you can grow and hunt. It's either that, or go hungry.

I told you earlier that Gray was me and Terry's cousin. He was a few years older than us, but the three of us had always been close. He drove a dump truck as a freelance owner-operator. Most recently, he'd had a lot of work, contracting out to the big windmill farm they're building to the west. Lots of hours. Lots of miles. Lots of money. You might think he was doing better financially than the rest of us were, and on paper, it sure looked that way. But being self-employed, Gray had no health insurance, and being five years shy of turning fifty, he was beginning to have all the problems that come with that. Being an owner-operator, he was responsible for the repairs, insurance, and upkeep on his truck, none of which was cheap. He also paid a ridiculous amount in child support each month for his two kids, both of which he'd had later in life. Now look, I'm all for paying child support. I think it's your responsibility as a parent. But it's also got to be within reason. Gray's ex-wife had gotten a really good lawyer (paid for by her parents, both of whom worked for the state government and had money). When court was all said and done, Gray was paying over twelve hundred dollars a month for two children! He loved his kids, and he never missed a payment, and he never truly complained about it. But at the same time, he was eating a lot of ramen noodles and cheap pasta and frozen pizzas just to get by.

Mattie had graduated with Gray, but like my older cousin, we'd known him all our lives. He was best friends with Seymour, which sometimes cause tension between him and Cecil. He earned a living by going around to old, abandoned farms and houses (of which there are a lot of in West Virginia), as well as yard sales and garage sales, and scavenging all the old farm equipment and furniture and other knick-knacks he could find. He'd then load it all into his pick-up truck and take it to Lewisburg or White Sulphur Springs and sell it to the antique dealers there, who would then mark the junk up to insanely high prices and sell it to rich folks vacationing from out-of-state. He also scavenged copper wire, scrap metal, aluminum cans—anything he could sell to the recycling center. His girlfriend worked at a daycare center in Frankfurt, and between the two of them, they were able to afford a small trailer on a plot of land out near Seymour's place. Mattie was quiet. Folks who didn't know him often mistook that silence for stand-offishness, but that wasn't the case. He just seldom had anything to say, and was usually content to just listen and go with the flow.

Anyway, that evening, like I said, we were all hanging out at Terry's place. His kids were out in the backyard, playing with Nerf guns. His wife was inside, watching television. And we were gathered around his old John Deere tractor, watching Terry work on the engine and offering him all sorts of unsolicited advice on how to do that while also commiserating on our unanimous financial desperation.

Terry loaded a pinch of tobacco into his bottom lip, and stared out across the yard at the kids.

"They're growing fast," Gray observed.

Terry stuffed his tobacco can in his back pocket and nodded. "Yeah, they are. We'd like to start a college fund for them both, but by the end of the month, we've only got like an extra ten dollars. I don't reckon that would pay for much by the time they graduated."

"No," I agreed, "it wouldn't. I'm in the same boat. Alicia is supposed to go off to Morgantown. She's already been accepted, but I still don't exactly know how I'm gonna pay for all of that."

"Scholarships," Darnell said. "Or look into government grants."

"Sure," I replied. "She got a small scholarship, and maybe she'll even qualify for some of those grants. The paperwork takes a long while to process. I talked to a fella over in Frankfurt who said his son's grant wasn't approved until the boy was a sophomore in college. In the meantime, there's dorm and books and . . . "

I shook my head and sighed.

Terry picked up a socket wrench and leaned over the tractor's engine. "Shit ain't right."

"No," Darnell said, "it's not. My boy wants to join the military after graduation next year. I'm ashamed to say it, but I felt sort of relieved when he told me that."

"Relieved?" Cecil frowned. "You ashamed of the military?"

"Not at all," Darnell said. "But all these wars now . . . it ain't like when we were growing up. How many years we been in Afghanistan? And how many times are we going to go back to Iraq? I don't like the thought of him getting shipped off like that."

"So you'd rather we be living under Sharia law?" Cecil asked. "Maybe those ISIS fuckers can set up shop over in Renick? It's better our guys go over there than they come here."

"Our guys?" Darnell took a long sip of beer. "I'm talking about my son, Cecil. How many kids you have again? Oh, that's right. None. Because ain't nobody wants to fuck you."

"Fuck you, Darnell."

"No thanks. I don't want to fuck you either."

Gray laughed, and then turned to Terry. "Take that ten bucks per month and put it in a savings account for them. It might not be much, but at least it's something."

"Hold up." Cecil held up a hand. "I'm still confused by what Darnell said."

"How's that?" Darnell asked.

"You said you were ashamed to feel relieved that your son wants to join the military, but then it sounded like you didn't want him joining the military. So, which is it?"

"It's both," Darnell explained. "No, I don't want

him to join the military. But I'm also sort of relieved that if he does, I wont have to try to figure out how to pay for college. That's where the shame part comes in. But I reckon you wouldn't know anything about that."

A hawk called overhead, circling the field.

"You got college funds for your kids?" Terry asked Gray.

"Hell, no. With what I pay in child support? But I do worry about it."

"Shit, boys." Donny groaned, easing himself out of a lawn chair and shuffling over to the cooler to fish out another beer. He popped the tab, sucked off the foam, and took a long drink. Then he sighed again.

"Enjoying my beer?" Terry asked.

Donny shrugged. "Y'all shouldn't worry about college so much. I mean, I didn't go to college and I turned out okay."

"Yeah," Terry said, "you're doing just fine."

Donny walked back to his chair. Terry glanced at me and rolled his eyes. I stifled a grin.

"We ought to become drug dealers," Seymour said, "like those guys in that show."

"Breaking Bad?" Mattie asked.

"Yeah," Seymour said. "That's the one."

Darnell shook his head. "Didn't work out too well for them, did it?"

"Spoilers, Darnell," Terry grunted, working the socket wrench. "I ain't watched it yet."

"Man, Breaking Bad ended back in twenty thirteen, Terry. You can't call spoilers on something that old! That's like getting mad because somebody told you Darth Vader was Luke Skywalker's father."

"It ain't that far-fetched," Gray said.

I turned to my older cousin. He had a strange expression on his face.

"What, that Darth Vader was Luke's father?"

He play punched me in the arm. "No, what Seymour said."

I frowned. "About us becoming drug dealers?"

"We could cook meth," Gray said. "You know up past Auto where the road ends and the National Forest begins?"

We all nodded.

"Well," Gray continued, "there's a trailer up there where they cook meth."

"I know the place you're talking about," Mattie said. "They nearly shot me last year when I was up that way hauling junk. Didn't think anybody lived in that trailer. Boy, was I surprised."

"How'd you get away?" Seymour asked.

Mattie shrugged. "Talked my way out of it. But Gray is right. They're definitely cooking meth there."

"And they're living pretty good as a result," Gray said.

"If they're doing so good for themselves," Cecil asked, "then how come they're living in a trailer?"

"They don't live there. They just cook meth there. They live in White Sulphur Springs, down by the Greenbrier."

Each of us fell silent for a moment. That area was one of the wealthiest parts of the state, or at least what passed for wealth in West Virginia. Home prices there were much higher than in our small town.

"Okay," I said, and I was just joking around at the time, but now I wish I hadn't. "So, how would we go about it? Ain't one of us who knows anything about how to cook meth."

"It's all on the internet," Gray said.

"What?" Terry stopped working on the engine and turned to us. "You mean like a YouTube video or something?"

"Trust me, cousin," Gray replied. "It's on there."

"I know that's right," Darnell agreed. "We got those child safety filters on our computer, but you wouldn't believe the shit that gets past it."

"Where would we get the chemicals?" I asked.

Gray made a sweeping gesture with his hands. "We've got two farmers, two guys who work at Walmart, and me."

"You?" Terry spat tobacco juice onto the gravel driveway. "What do you have?"

"Access to construction sites, where the chemicals are. I reckon between all of us, we can get our hands on whatever we'd need."

"I can help, too," Donny offered from his chair.

"That all sounds good," I said, "but where would we cook? All of us have families, except for Donny. I reckon ain't none of us making that shit at home."

"You ain't doing it at my place, neither," Donny said. "The government has special cameras on planes and satellites that can see that shit."

"I think those register heat from lights at growing operations," Darnell said.

"No," Cecil argued, "he's right. They can detect meth, too. Hell, ain't much they can't detect at this point."

"Well, then that's that." I paused and took a sip of beer. "We don't have anywhere to build a lab."

Terry spoke quietly. "What about down yonder in great-grandaddy's hollow?"

Gray grinned. "Shit, that's perfect!"

"Why?" Seymour asked.

"Because nobody ever goes there," Gray explained. "The terrain is too rugged for hunters, and the trees grow all close together the deeper inside you get. Plus, it's riddled with sinkholes and caves. Easy way to break your leg or get bit by a snake. You ever been inside it, Terry?"

He shook his head. "Nope. Closest I've been to the hollow is the field next to it. I used to graze the cattle down there, but I stopped after I lost a few of them."

"Coyotes?" Donny asked.

Terry shrugged. "I reckon? It was the damnedest thing. Two young calves. Disappeared within a week of each other. Never found a trace of them. I reckon maybe they wandered down into the hollow, but I had my hands full and never found out for sure. The rest of the herd stopped grazing that area, and I don't use it no more."

"Well, if it's that hard to get in and out of, then how would we build a lab there?" Cecil asked.

"We wouldn't have to," Gray said. "Terry, you've still got that old camper, right?"

"You mean Papaw's old pop up? Yeah. The kids play in it sometimes, but other than that, we don't use it. That thing is older than we are. I've got it parked down yonder."

"We could haul it down there with the tractor," Gray said. "Sure, the trees grow close together, but I reckon we could find a path. If not, we could make a path and a clearing. Wouldn't take us more than a day to clear out the brush."

I couldn't help but notice the excitement in Gray's voice. It bothered me, but I couldn't resist further expanding on the idea, because if anything, it was the most interesting discussion the eight of us had had in quite some time. It beat talking about politics or sports again.

"Say we do all that," I said. "What then? How do we sell it?"

"Frank's right," Darnell agreed. "Not for nothing, but everyone and their granny already has all the meth hook-ups they need around here. The competition would be something fierce."

"We don't sell it here," Gray said. "We don't shit where we eat."

"Then where do we sell it?" I asked.

"I'm running loads back and forth to Maryland, Pennsylvania, and Virginia every week. Got one scheduled for New Jersey next week, too. People in those states got a lot more money than folks around here do."

Terry's wife came out of the house then and called him and the kids to supper. She invited the rest of us, as well. Gray and Donny accepted the offer, but Darnell, the Peters brothers, Mattie, and myself bowed out.

When we left, the sun was just sinking beneath the horizon.

By the time I got home, it was full dark.

Alicia was busy doing her homework at the kitchen table. Since it was so late, I asked her if a frozen pizza would be okay for dinner. She thought that sounded fine, so I popped one in the oven and then sat down with her and asked about her day. We talked for a good ten minutes, and I could tell there was something bothering her. After a bit, I coaxed it out of her.

"Daddy," she asked, "how would you feel if I didn't go to school after graduation?"

"Well," I said, trying to hide my shock, "what would you do instead, honey?"

"Sally Coleman got a job at the hair salon in Lewisburg. The money is good and they're helping her with beautician school. I guess they pay for part of it out of your wages. She says they're looking to hire more people."

"Is that something you want to do? What about Biometrics?"

Her expression grew sad. "Biometrics could wait. If I took the job, then maybe I could save up enough money for college."

I put my hand over hers, and gave it a squeeze, and tried to talk around the lump in my throat.

"Don't you worry about that," I said. "College is all taken care of."

"How? I've heard you on the phone the other night. Mom's life insurance has just about run out."

"It's okay." I smiled. "I have a plan. Dad is gonna take care of everything."

Later that night, after I was sure that Alicia was asleep, I called Gray. Then, I put him on hold and dialed in Terry. Once I'd merged the calls and had all three of us on the line together, I told them what I was thinking.

That was on a Tuesday night. The next Sunday, the eight of us gathered at Terry's place and went to check out the hollow for ourselves.

FOUR

IT WAS AROUND ten in the morning by the time I got to Terry's place. Gray, Mattie and the Peters brothers were already there. We would have met up earlier, but since it was Sunday, Cecil and Seymour had gone to church first, and Mattie had slept in.

I pulled in behind Gray's truck. The six of us stood out in the yard, drinking cheap coffee and waiting for Darnell and Donny to arrive. Terry's cows mooed out in the field. Some crows cawed from the nearby treetops. A distant buzzing came from the five beehives Terry had positioned out between his apple trees. A deer stood nearby, staring at the apple trees, and then the hives, and then us, trying to decide if snatching some of those white apple blossoms was worth the double risk. It was one of those cool West Virginia mornings, where the fog from the night before still hovers over the ground like a thin blanket, but by noon will be burned off by the heat. I don't know. I'm not a poet. But all of those things are why I love living here. Ain't no place like it in the world, I imagine.

We heard the crunch of tires on gravel, and then a car we didn't recognize turned in to Terry's driveway—a Dodge Neon that was mostly piss-yellow, except for the driver's side front panel, which was black. The thing belched smoke out the tailpipe, and sat so low that the undercarriage scraped against the driveway as it pulled in.

"Is that . . . " Terry squinted. "Darnell and Donny?"

"Looks like it," Seymour replied, "but that ain't Darnell's car."

"No," Mattie agreed. "It sure ain't."

The engine stopped and the doors opened and sure enough, Darnell got out of the driver's side and Donny exited from the passenger's seat. Darnell paused, glaring at all of us.

"What are y'all staring at?"

"Just wondering whose car that is." I explained.

"It's my neighbor's. Mine wouldn't start this morning. The alternator's shot, and I can't get it fixed until next payday, so I'm borrowing this. My neighbor lost his license because of another DUI, so he can't drive it anyway. Promised him a case of beer after I get paid."

"Shit," Cecil said. "I'd rent me a car before I'd be seen driving around in that."

"If I can't afford to get the alternator fixed, how the hell could I afford to rent a car, Cecil?"

"You boys want coffee?" Terry asked.

Darnell held up a travel mug. "No, thanks. Brought my own."

"I wouldn't say no to a cup," Donny replied.

After Terry had gotten him squared away, and we were all caffeinated, we headed off for the hollow. We took Terry's pick-up truck, because it had four-wheel

26

drive and we'd definitely need that, given the terrain. Terry, Gray and me all sat up front in the cab. The others piled into the bed. We drove down the rutted dirt road that winds through the farm, and Terry had some fun hitting the bumps and making the guys in the back bounce and curse as they spilled their coffees. The truck didn't have Bluetooth, but it did have a CD player, and Gray and I sang along to Shooter Jennings's "Outlaw You." I don't care for a lot of modern country music. It sounds too much like pop to me. But I do like his stuff.

Every time we came to a fence, Donny would climb down from the back of the truck and open the gate, and then climb back up after we'd driven through.

"Make sure you latch them tight," Terry warned. "I don't need my cows getting out."

"I'm on it," Donny said, tipping his camouflage ballcap.

Eventually, we headed out into an open field, and Terry drove slower and slower, guiding the truck up and down the rolling, rocky hills. Eventually the terrain became too rough even for the four-wheel drive, so he put it in park and shut the engine off.

"Guess we'll have to walk from here," he said, pulling out his tobacco can and loading up a pinch.

"Reckon so," I agreed.

"This truck won't make it all the way?" Cecil asked.

"Not without breaking an axle," Terry replied.

Cecil sat his empty coffee mug on the tailgate. "Serves you right for buying a Chevy. Should have bought a Dodge."

"Motherfucker," Darnell said, "just twenty minutes ago, you were making fun of the Dodge me and Donny pulled up in."

"That wasn't a Dodge Ram," Cecil explained. "It was a—"

"Come on," I interrupted. "It'll be noon soon. Let's get a move on before it gets too hot."

We started up the hill, wading through the tall grass and weeds. Pretty soon our boots and pants legs were wet with the leftover morning dew. I glanced down and spotted a little deer tick scurrying up my calf, and flicked him away.

"Ticks are bad this year," Donny said.

We all nodded in agreement that they were.

"Filthy little bloodsuckers," Seymour said. "Ever wonder why God made something like them? I mean, they don't eat nothing but blood, and they spread disease. Why put them here on Earth?"

Gray paused to light a cigarette. "I reckon He put them here so that we'd have something to bitch about."

"Hey, Terry," Donny said, "let me get a pinch of snuff?"

Terry eyed him with uncertainty. "You been picking your nose today?"

"No."

Terry hesitated. "Okay. But just one pinch. I ain't got but the one can. The rest of the roll is back at the house."

After about twenty minutes of going up and down the hills, we reached the summit of one particular mound and there was the hollow, spread out below us. The hillsides around it were pretty devoid of trees—just a few saplings here and there. But the hollow itself was choked with them. It stretched for maybe a quarter of a mile—a sprawling tangle of pine and oak and maples and birch, all growing so close together that I doubt the sun had hit the forest floor in decades.

"Jesus," Seymour said, "ain't that a spooky looking place?"

"Our great-granddaddy thought so," Terry said.

Gray and I glanced at each other, and then back to our cousin.

"How so?" Gray asked.

"Y'all remember when I found his recipes for moonshine?"

We nodded.

"Well," Terry said, "he wrote in there about how he only come here during the day. Never at night. He thought it was haunted. Remember that, Frank?"

I nodded. "That's right. He did. I'd forgotten about that part."

Seymour frowned. "If he thought it was haunted, then why did he put his still in the hollow?"

Terry shrugged. "I reckon everybody else in these parts back then thought the place was haunted, too. He figured nobody would be fool enough to come messing around with it. And he was right."

Gray nodded. "Mom sure didn't like this spot much. I remember her talking about how they avoided it growing up."

"Yeah," I agreed, "I remember my dad telling me that, too. And they never let us play here either, when we were kids. But I always figured that had something to do with the still. Not because of ghosts."

"Well," Darnell said, "let's take a look."

"Are we really doing this?" Donny asked. "I mean, are we really gonna scout out a place to cook meth? Are we serious about this?"

We all glanced at one another, but nobody spoke. Then, Gray cleared his throat.

"We're already here, right? And ain't none of us ever explored it. Even if we're not going to cook meth, it's something to do on a Sunday afternoon. What else did you have planned?"

Donny shrugged. "I was gonna do a puzzle later. Maybe watch a movie. But that's all."

Gray turned around and started down the slope.

We followed after him.

"Wasn't this all forest at one point?" Seymour asked.

"It was," I told him, "but they logged most of that out back when our great-grandaddy was still alive. It's just the hollow now. Everything else is hills and fields."

After a few minutes, we reached the edge of the hollow. The trees loomed up over us, casting shadows on the grass. The ground here was dry, as if the roots had sucked up all of the leftover morning dew. I peered into the shadows. It wasn't full dark, under those leaves. Sunlight fell in places, but only in patches. The undergrowth was unbelievably thick— lots of thorn bushes, ferns, pine saplings, and vines and such. Making our way through it would be exhausting and possibly dangerous.

"Pretty thick in there," I said, noticing that my voice sounded odd this close to the small patch of forest. "It's gonna be hard going."

"A lot of ticks," Mattie said. "And probably snakes."

"There's a game trail over here." Gray pointed. "We can follow that."

We gathered around him and looked. A small path did indeed lead into the hollow, although it looked seldom-used. There were no fresh hoofprints, and weeds had started to grow up through the dirt.

"We'll have to go single file," Cecil said.

I nodded in agreement.

"Look there," Donny said. "Wild garlic."

We looked at where he was pointing, and sure enough, there was wild garlic growing in clumps right at the edge of the hollow. I glanced in each direction, and spotted more.

"How about that?" I said. "Looks like it rings the entire hollow. Look at it spread out like that."

Darnell nodded. "It's everywhere! Too bad it's not ginseng root. We'd have a nice little fortune on our hands."

"We still could," Gray said.

Darnell frowned. "From garlic?"

"No, from meth."

Donny knelt by a patch of wild garlic, pulled out his pocketknife, and proceeded to dig up a clump. Then he brushed the dirt off of it and peeled the clove and popped it into his mouth whole. I could smell it from where I stood—sharp and tart.

"You ain't getting any more of my snuff," Terry warned. "Not with those fingers. The tobacco will taste like garlic!"

Donny chewed, grimaced, and then grinned.

"It's fresh alright," he said. "Burns a little."

"No shit it's fresh," Cecil muttered. "I can smell it from here. Ain't no wonder you don't have a girlfriend."

Ignoring him, Donny looked up at Terry. "Okay with you if I dig some of this up on the way back out?"

Terry shrugged. "Sure. But what the hell are you going to do with all that wild garlic?"

"Sell it." Donny grinned, and there were pieces of garlic in his teeth. "While the rest of y'all cook meth, I'll be a garlic baron."

We laughed at that, and then fell quiet. In the stillness, it occurred to me that the birds and insects had gotten quiet, too. I figured it was because of our presence.

"Okay," Gray said. "Let's get a move on. The Powers are playing in Charelston tonight, and I want to be home in time to listen to the game."

"You and that minor league baseball," Cecil said.

"It ain't my fault we don't have no major league teams," Gray said. "Anyway, come on."

But Gray didn't move. He hesitated, clearly waiting for one of us to go first. Instead, we all stared at him. He frowned, snuffed his cigarette out on the sole of his boot, and then shrugged.

"Fuck it," he said. "I'll lead the way."

I grinned. Terry fell in behind Gray. Then Cecil and Seymour, followed by Mattie. Donny and Darnell started in after them. And I brought up the rear. I was still smiling as the forest closed overtop of us.

Thinking back on it now, that was the last time I really smiled.

FIVE

HE FIRST THING I noticed was how quiet the woods in the hollow were. There should have been birds overhead, chirping and flying and warning each other—and the rest of the wildlife— about our presence. There should have been bugs—gnats and mosquitoes buzzing our faces, and butterflies rushing about, and ants and caterpillars crawling around on the dead leaves carpeting the forest floor. There should most certainly have been squirrels up in the trees. But there was nothing. Not even a stray tick. I'd noticed how quiet and lifeless things seemed on the edge of the hollow. That seemed to hold true for inside its perimeter, as well.

And yet, it wasn't completely lifeless. There was the vegetation, of course, so thick and jumbled that it made for slow going as we walked down the game trail. And there were other signs that life had passed through this place, too. I saw an occasional faded print in the dirt. One was a deer and the other belonged to either a coyote or a stray dog. I spotted a few black walnuts and acorns that had obviously been chewed open by a squirrel or some other small animal. A few times I saw dried bird shit splattered across leaves. That all indicated to me that wildlife did indeed sometimes venture into this hollow. The question was why didn't they stick around? It couldn't just be because we were here. There had to be something else to it.

"Wish we'd have brought some guns," I said.

"Why?" Darnell asked. "We ain't hunting."

"No, but . . . " I hesitated, sighed, and then quickly explained my observations to them. I figured they'd all make fun of me, tell me that the old ghost stories were getting to me, and that I sounded like my great-grandaddy, but they didn't.

"Could be a bear," Donny said. "They sometimes have that effect on the other animals."

"Yeah." Terry nodded. "I reckon that might be it. Did y'all see that ridge up yonder when we come in, just to the left of the hollow?"

We nodded.

He spat tobacco juice and continued. "I spotted a big old black bear at the top of that ridge last fall. Meant to come back and see if I could bag her later, but I never saw her again. I'll bet she's denned up somewhere in here."

"It would be a good spot for a bear," Gray agreed. "We'll have to watch ourselves. Make lots of noise and such, so we don't surprise her."

"Fuck that noise," Darnell said. "I ain't traipsing around in a hollow where there's a bear. I got chased by one when I was little. I'm never going through that again."

"Relax." Cecil bent down and pulled up his pants leg, revealing a handgun holstered to his ankle, just above the top of his muddy, weather-beaten work boot. "I've got my Sig-Sauer with me."

"That ain't no rifle," Seymour said.

"No," Cecil agreed with his brother, "it ain't. But it's got more than enough stopping power to kill a full-grown bear. All I've got to do is hit her."

"We've seen you shoot," Gray teased. "Easier said than done."

"Fuck you." Grinning, Cecil rolled his pants leg back down.

"Maybe we ought to come back another time," Donny suggested. "When we're better prepared."

"We're fine," Gray said. "Look, we're already here. We might as well keep going. All kidding around aside, if there is a bear in this hollow, Cecil's pistol is more than enough to stop it. And we all know that unless she has cubs or unless we surprise her, that old bear is going to run off and hide before we ever even see her. Let's just finish looking around."

"Looking around for what?" Darnell gestured at the forest. "This narrow ass deer trail is the only way in and out that we've found. Now, I don't know what all we need to set up a meth lab, but I damn sure reckon it's a lot more equipment than we can fit down this path."

"Not if we widen the trail," Gray said. "We can come in here with some brush hogs and chainsaws. Terry's got his tractor, and me and Seymour have four wheelers."

"My ATV has a busted rear axle," Seymour replied. "Can't afford to get it fixed."

"Be that as it may, we can widen this path easily enough."

"Enough to get Terry's camper down here?" Mattie asked. "I don't know about that. Darnell is right. This is awfully rugged terrain."

"We'll find a way," Gray insisted. "I'm telling you boys, this could work. We wouldn't have to worry about money no more. Isn't that what we want?"

"I sure do," Donny said quietly.

"Sure," I replied, "it would be nice to not have to worry about money. I told y'all about Alicia and college. But I just don't know that this is the way, Gray. It was sort of funny when we were all bullshitting about it the other night, and I'll admit, when I got home, I considered the possibility. That's why I called you and Terry later that night. But now that we're here . . . ?"

He turned away from us, shoulders set, and started down the trail again. Terry reached out and grabbed his shoulder and gently spun him back around.

"Gray," he said, "me, you and Frank . . . well, the three of us have been cousins a long time."

"Since we were born," I added.

"We know each other pretty well," Terry continued, "and I know right now that there's something you ain't telling us. I've known it since you brought this up on Tuesday night. There's more to it. What's going on? And don't bullshit us."

He stared evenly at me and Terry, and then in turn at each of the others. Then, his shoulders slumped, and he sighed. He shook a cigarette out of his pack, lit it, inhaled, and then sighed again.

"You boys know I've been making runs up north, to Maryland and Pennsylvania and the like."

We nodded.

"Well, there's this strip bar in Pennsylvania, near the hotel where I stay. It's called The Odessa. It's right off the Interstate—the hotel, I mean—so it's easy for me to just get up and go in the morning. The strip club sits back a little ways from it."

Darnell groaned. "You knocked up a stripper, didn't you?"

"No." Gray shook his head. "Nothing like that."

"Well, what then?" I asked.

"The fellas who own the strip club, they're Russians. As in the Russian mob. Nice guys, but I owe them some money."

"The Russian mob are nice guys?" Terry asked. "For Pete's sake, Gray . . . "

"They are! For the most part. Sounds like the previous owner, some guy they called Whitey, was a lot meaner. They sort of remind me of us, you know? Just normal guys."

"Who you just happen to be in debt to," Darnell said.

"How much?" I asked. "How much do you owe them?"

"Quite a bit," Gray replied. "More than I can pay. But we got to talking, and if I do this—if I set up this operation and handle transportation and distribution, they're willing to wipe the slate clean. They'll even send down some guys to teach us how to make it."

"Fuck this," Darnell said. "I'm out."

"You want us to get in bed with the Russian mob?" I took a step toward him, fists clenching. "What the fuck is wrong with you, Gray? We've got kids. *You've* got kids!"

"You're goddamned right I do," he yelled, "and it's killing me! It's killing me not having any goddamned money left over at the end of the month. And it's killing you guys, too. Each and every last one of you. You said so yourselves the other night."

"Maybe so," I shouted, "but this ain't the way! I want no part of this bullshit."

He shrugged. "Well, it's too late for me to say no, Frank. You guys can do whatever you want, but I'm already committed to doing it. I'm supposed to check in with them next week, when I make my next run up north."

"We should go to the cops," Cecil said. "Tell them what's going on."

"The cops can't do shit," Gray said. "These guys own the cops. They own everything. Soon as we did that, they'd know about it, and then we'd be dead."

"I thought they were nice guys," I taunted.

"They might kill you," Darnell said, "but not me. I already told you—I'm out. I want nothing to do with any of this shit. This ain't got anything to do with me!"

"That's easy for you," Gray replied. "I can't just walk away. I'm already in too deep."

"That's on you," Darnell said.

"Look . . . " Gray took a long drag off his cigarette. "I'm sorry I wasn't honest with all of you. Seriously, I am. I just reckoned it was something we could all do together—a way for all of us to finally make some real money. If you guys don't want to be a part of it, I understand. No hard feelings. But I've got to do this. Y'all head on back to Terry's. I'll finish checking things out here by myself and then meet you back there."

He turned away again and started back down the trail. We all watched him go, and then we looked at each other.

"Wait," Terry called.

Gray paused and turned around again. "What? You gonna hit me?"

"No," Terry said, "I'm coming with you. Don't get me wrong. I'm pissed as shit at you right now, Gray. But you're family, so . . . what choice do I have?"

I nodded, hating myself for it. "He's right. You've done some fucked up shit in your life, Gray, but this? This tops them all."

"I know. I'm sorry."

"Save your apologies. I need you to understand how angry I am right now."

"I understand. You don't have to help."

"Yes," I said, "I do. Terry is right. Family is family."

"I ain't got no family except y'all," Donny said. "I'll come, too."

We all stood quiet for a moment. Then Cecil kicked a root jutting up out of the dirt and looked at us, and shoved his hands in his pockets.

"I reckon y'all made enough noise to scare that bear away," he said, "but just in case, I'll come along. You might need my gun. Mind you, I ain't signing on to working with the Russians, but I'll help you with this part today. Fair?"

Gray nodded.

"Well," Seymour said, "I go where my little brother goes, so yeah, I'll stick around."

"Me, too," Mattie said.

One by one, we all turned to Darnell. He stared at us, and then shook his head.

"Fucking white people," he muttered. "All y'all are fucking crazy."

Gray grinned. "Does that mean you're coming with us?"

"I'm fixing to knock that stupid hat off your head when we're through," Darnell said, "but yeah, I guess I'm coming along."

We started down the trail again. Like before, Gray was in the lead, followed by Terry, Cecil, Seymour, Mattie, Donny, Darnell and then me. Unlike before, we walked mostly in silence, not speaking to one another. I tried to shuffle my feet loud enough, just in case there was a bear holed up somewhere ahead.

The trees grew even closer together over us, filtering out the sunlight. I pulled out my phone to check the time, and discovered that there was no cellular service in the hollow. That wasn't a surprise. West Virginia's topography has always allowed for shitty cell coverage. What was a surprise was the time. It was only early afternoon, but given how tight the vegetation was, the illumination was like evening in the hollow.

It grew even darker as we continued on.

SIX

ABOUT FORTY-FIVE MINUTES to an hour had gone by when we found a flat area that Gray thought would suffice for the lab set-up. But that was also when we found the bear.

Or, I should say that was also when we found what was *left* of the bear.

We'd stopped in a part of the hollow that had surely been a clearing at some point in the past. The ground was flat and wide, but it was also choked with stunted saplings and thickets of brier bushes. A trifecta of poison ivy, poison oak and poison sumac was trying to overrun the place in a battle for supremacy against the other plants—and the trio was winning.

I sat down on a log. Normally, if you do that in the woods, it's an invitation for ants and other bugs living beneath the dead bark to come out and climb all over you, but that didn't happen. Darnell and Donny sat down on either side of me. Cecil plopped down on a nearby rock, and Seymour leaned up against a gnarled oak tree growing on the outskirts of the former clearing. Terry and Gray remained standing. Terry hooked a finger into his mouth and got rid of his dip. Then he pulled out his tobacco can and put in a fresh one. Gray lit a cigarette and looked around, surveying the area.

"I reckon this would work. If we widen the trail a little on both sides, we could get equipment in here. Wouldn't take but a few days or so to clear out all this brush."

"I'm not fucking with that poison ivy," Cecil said. "I'm deathly allergic to it."

"You ain't special," Darnell said. "Everybody's allergic to poison ivy."

"We're not," I said, nodding at my two cousins.

"How's that?" Donny asked.

I shrugged. "When we were little, our parents wanted to take a ride out to the end of Shale Bank Road and have a picnic. They left our granddaddy to babysit the three of us."

Terry nodded, chuckling. "Not too far from here. His home place was over on the ridge. I'll show y'all on the way back. The foundations should be visible after we get out of this hollow."

"Didn't your grandpa lock you in the chicken house once, Frank?" Darnell asked.

I nodded. "Yes, he did. He wasn't much of a babysitter, truth be told. Locked me in the chicken house once. And there was another time, Gray and I got in a fight when we were little, and he handed Gray a sickle and me an axe and told us to go down by the springhouse and fight it out."

Darnell's eyes widened. "Did you?"

"Hell, no!" Gray laughed. "We spent the rest of the afternoon pretending we were He-Man and Skeletor."

"I'll be back," Donny said, doing a terrible Arnold Schwarzenegger impression.

"You're thinking Conan the Barbarian," I told him.

"And the Terminator," Darnell added.

"Anyway," I continued, "the day our parents went on the picnic, Grandaddy made us soup. Supposedly, he put one poison ivy leaf in it. He said we'd be immune to poison ivy after that."

"That's some bullshit," Cecil said.

I shrugged. "Maybe. Grandaddy was prone to bullshit. And I damn sure wouldn't give Alicia poison ivy to eat. But I will say, ain't none of us ever had poison ivy. Maybe a little itch here or there, but not like when other folks get it."

Gray and Terry nodded in agreement.

"That's fucked up," Darnell murmured. "It's abuse."

"Yeah," I agreed, "it is. Like I said, he wasn't much of a babysitter."

Gray waded into the undergrowth, and I could tell by his expression that he was envisioning how it would look after he'd set the lab up. Then, his expression slowly changed. He stared at something intently.

"What's wrong?" I stood up.

He pointed. "There's a skeleton. No, wait . . . *skeletons*."

We all hurried over to where he stood. Cecil, Seymour, Donny and Darnell made a point of keeping clear of the poison ivy. Briers tugged at my pants leg, nicking me with thorns. Sure enough, there were five skeletons spread out on the ground. The vegetation hadn't concealed them completely yet, and while all of the flesh was gone, there were still a few matted tufts of fur. The biggest skeleton was a bear. The other four scattered around it were smaller.

"There's your bear, Terry," I said, "but those other four . . . are those dogs?"

"Coyotes." He spat a stream of brown tobacco juice onto the ground. "You can tell by their skulls. Judging by their state, I'd say all five of them have been here since last fall."

"The hell?" Darnell bent over, peering closer. "What happened to them?"

Terry shook his head. "If I had to guess? I reckon the bear died in here, and then when it was rotting, the smell attracted the coyotes."

"But what killed the bear?" Donny asked.

"A hunter probably shot him out yonder," Seymour suggested, "but couldn't track him down in this hollow."

"No," Terry said, "I'd have known about that. Other than you fellas, there's only a few people I let hunt on my land. If one of them had tagged this bear, they would have told me."

"Poacher?" Cecil asked.

Terry shook his head again. "No, I'd have heard the shot."

"Maybe it was sick," Darnell said. "Crawled up in here and died."

We all nodded in agreement that it was the most likely scenario. All of us except Donny, that is.

"Well," he said, "if that's so, then what killed the coyotes?"

None of us responded, because none of us had an answer.

Finally, Darnell said, "Well, if the bear was sick, and the coyotes ate its carcass, then maybe they got sick, too."

"And died right here next to it?" Donny frowned. "That would have to be a real quick sort of disease."

We all looked around, as if expecting the hollow to give us the answers. It didn't.

Terry frowned, stroking his chin.

"What are you thinking about?" I asked.

"Them two calves I lost. Remember, I told you about them? They were grazing on the outskirts of this place. You reckon they wandered in here and . . . "

"And what?"

He shrugged. "I don't know."

Cecil's eyes widened, and he pointed at a particularly thick tangle of purple and green briers. "Well, would you look at that!"

We all turned our attention to where he was indicating, and squinted. After a moment, I saw it. There was a small cave entrance there in the ground, just big enough for a human to crawl through. That in itself was no surprise. West Virginia is absolutely riddled with caves. Seriously. You throw a rock here, and you're bound to hit a cave. They run under the state like honeycomb in a beehive.

The problem was Seymour. Ever since we were kids, Seymour had loved himself some caves. He was nuts about them. Growing up, he was forever exploring them. He'd skip school because he was off in a cave somewhere. It got to be that he'd trespass on other people's properties, because the cave systems would bring him out there. One time he disappeared into a cavern down by the Greenbrier River, and they sent in a search party for him, but while they were inside looking for him, Seymour came out elsewhere. Then he went in and let the search party know he was okay. If I remember correctly, he was grounded for six months after that, and his folks had to pay a fine. Soon after, the state dynamited the cave entrance while they were widening the road and building the Keene Memorial Bridge. For several years after high school, Seymour had a job working at Lost World Caverns over in Lewisburg, but it didn't pay but minimum wage, and he'd eventually had to give it up. I sometimes think he was more heartbroken about that than anything else that had happened in his life. He had a shed out back of his house where he displayed the things he'd found in the local caves over the years—Native American arrowheads and axe heads, fossils of plants and tiny animals, bullets and buttons from the Civil War, snake skeletons, and all kinds of other stuff. He'd bought himself some glass showcases from a jewelry store that was going out of business, and he displayed his artifacts in those. He loved showing them off, and talking about where he'd discovered them. If things had been different, if Seymour had the opportunity to go to college and earn a degree, he could have probably made a living as a cave explorer, doing something he was passionate about.

Instead, it had remained just a hobby for him.

But a hobby he was no less excited about, whenever the opportunity presented itself.

"Seymour," I said, already knowing what he was thinking, "maybe you ought not to go poking your head in there."

If he heard me, he gave no indication. Instead, he broke a large branch off a nearby sapling, and then used it to beat back the briers and vines. Green sap stuck to it like blood. I was reminded of what Donny had said just a few minutes earlier, about Conan the Barbarian. That's who Seymour looked like in that moment.

When he was finished, we all had a clearer view of the cave's mouth. It looked like it sloped down into the earth at an angle. Definitely not big enough to stand up in, but any one of us could have crawled through the opening with no problem.

"He's right," Darnell said. "Remote area like this hollow, it's probably full of rattlesnakes or copperheads, all denned up down there."

"Not this time of year," Seymour said. "Terry, lend me your phone?"

"Why?"

"Because I didn't bring mine with me, and I need a light."

"Nope." Terry shook his head. "The flashlight app on my phone kills the battery."

Seymour turned to Gray. "Can I borrow your lighter?"

Shrugging, Gray reached into his pocket, pulled out the lighter, and tossed it to Seymour, who caught it with one hand.

"Don't lose it," Gray warned. "All my others are at home."

Seymour turned back to the cave. His expression was eager and excited.

I grabbed his shirt sleeve. When he turned to look back at me, I shook my head.

"Leave it alone," I said. "It's just like every other cave you've ever been in. You're not going to see anything in there that you haven't seen a dozen times before."

Smiling, he pulled free of my grip. "That's where you're wrong. Each cave is different. That's one of the things I love about them. Each one tells its own story, and has its own surprises."

I turned to his brother and Mattie and gestured helplessly.

Cecil shrugged. "Ain't no talking him out of it. You know that. He likes caves the way most men like NASCAR."

"I hate to admit it," Mattie said, "but Cecil is right."

"I'll just take a quick look," Seymour promised. "Get an idea of how far down it goes. We can come back and explore it fully another time."

He knelt down on his knees, flicked the lighter, and poked his head inside the cave. Then, after a moment, he crawled inside. We saw the glow of the flame, but then that disappeared, too.

"It slopes down a good twenty yards," he called, "and then it looks like it levels out. Might be big enough for me to stand up in. I'm gonna go see."

"Be careful," Donny yelled.

There was about a minute of silence, and then Seymour called out again. This time, his voice sounded far away and muffled.

"Yep, it's big enough to stand up in. Stinks to high heaven, though. And it sure is dark. This lighter ain't doing much g—"

Then he screamed.

Gray's cigarette fell out of his mouth as he gasped.

"Get out of the way!" Cecil pushed past all of us, and dropped to the ground on his hands and knees. He shouted into the cave opening. "Seymour, what's happening? What's wrong?"

His brother screamed again. I'd never heard anything so terrible in my life—a high-pitched, long, drawn-out, warbling shriek that surely must have ruptured something inside of him, because human throats weren't meant to make that sort of sound. And just when it seemed like it was about to end, Seymour let loose with another one that was even higher in pitch—a sort of sputtering squeal. I'd heard pigs make a noise like that when they were being slaughtered.

Cecil pushed head first into the cave. Terry reached out and grabbed at his ankles, but Cecil kicked him away.

"Let go of me! Let me go, goddamn it! That's my brother in there."

Terry got a firmer hold on him and dragged him back out again. His red makeshift political hat fell off his head. As Cecil grabbed for it, Mattie pushed past us all and hurried into the tunnel.

"Mattie," I yelled. "Goddamn it!"

He vanished into the darkness. I bent down and peered inside. So did Donny, crouched to my right side. Terry sat nearby, restraining Cecil, who was cursing up a storm.

Then, Seymour stopped screaming, and we all fell quiet. I heard Mattie scuffling in the dark. There was no sign of the cigarette lighter that Seymour had taken with him.

"Let go of me, Terry," Cecil warned. "Goddamn it, I ain't playing!"

"Neither am I," Terry said, forcing him back down. "We don't know what's going on, and you ain't doing anybody any good rushing in there."

"Fuck this," Darnell said. "I'm calling nine one one."

"Why?" Gray asked.

Darnell pulled out his cell phone with one hand and gestured at the cave with the other.

"We don't even know what's happening yet," Gray said.

"All the more reason," Darnell argued. "Ain't nobody more experienced with crawling around in caves than Seymour is. Did you not hear him screaming? Whatever has happened is bad. I'm calling an ambulance, and then I'm calling the cops. Hell, I'll get the National Guard out here if I have to."

"The cops?" Gray's tone was panicked. "Now just hold up a minute. We don't need the police out here traipsing around Terry's land."

"You worried about your cousin's land, Gray, or are you worried about them finding out what we were up to?"

Gray stepped closer to Darnell. His posture stiffened. "What were we up to, Darnell? I don't know about you, but I was out here for a walk in the woods."

"Like hell."

"Both of you shut up," I snapped. "That's enough!"

Mattie called out, and like Seymour before him, his voice was muffled and seemed to come from beneath us. "Seymour, hang on! I'm coming. I'm coming, Seym—eeeep!"

The tunnel fell silent again. Somehow, that was more unnerving than the screams.

"Shit," Darnell muttered. "There's no phone signal down here."

"Mattie," I called. "Seymour?"

Donny crawled past me.

"Where are you going?" Terry asked.

"I'm going in after them," he said.

Before we could respond, Donny plunged headfirst into the cave. As I watched his boots slip into the darkness, I pulled out my own cell phone. Like Darnell, I had no service, but what I did have was a flashlight app.

"Y'all stay here," I said.

Gray opened his mouth to argue and I glared at him until he shut it. Then I turned and followed Donny into the cave. I held the phone out in front of me, illuminating the way. Behind me, I heard Cecil start struggling with Terry again. Then the sounds faded. It was hard navigating the tunnel on two knees and with only one free hand, but after about ten feet, the space widened a bit, and I was able to move in sort of a crouched, duck walk position. The passage sloped steadily downward at about a thirty-degree angle— gentle enough that we didn't fall or slide, but just steep enough that we were quickly deep under the earth.

"You hear anything?" I whispered.

"Maybe," Donny replied. "Something . . . wet? Maybe water dripping?"

Our voices sounded strange there underground. Even our whispers echoed. We continued on our way.

Eventually, the slope terminated in a broad, flat

area. Upon reaching it, both of us stood up slowly and worked the kinks and cramps out of our muscles. Donny drew a breath, and was about to call out, when I grasped his shoulder and squeezed. He turned back to me, and I held a finger to my lips.

I said earlier that Seymour's scream was the most awful sound I'd ever heard, but looking back now, I was wrong. His screams were the second most awful sound I ever heard.

The most awful was what we were hearing now. Greedy grunts. Low, murmuring growls. And loud, wet slurping sounds. I think that was the worst part of it—how *wet* the noises were.

Donny trembled beneath my touch. I was shaking too, as I swept the phone across the space, looking for the source of the sound. The flashlight beam glanced across Mattie's boots and then his pants legs, and then . . .

Donny screamed.

Both Seymour and Mattie lay on the floor of the cave. Mattie's left arm was sprawled across his best friend's chest. Both of them were dead. They had to be, given the state of their bodies. Their throats had been slashed wide open, as had their chests and their wrists. Mattie's ribs jutted from his midsection, and his guts were haphazardly strewn about the floor. The flashlight beam illuminated five humanish figures who were crouched over them, eagerly drinking from the wounds. One of them clutched Seymour's hand as you might do with a lover, and was sucking the open wound on his wrist like a kid sucking on a Slurpee straw. Startled by the sound of Donny's scream, they turned to us. All of them were naked and hairless.

Near as I could tell, they didn't even have eyebrows or eyelashes. Their skin was the color of milk. They were scrawny, with yellow, pupil-less eyes sunk deep in their skulls and their bones well-defined through their pallid skin. One of them hissed at us. Its face was slathered in Mattie's blood. Gray lips pulled back to reveal receded white gums lined with fangs. I didn't see molars or any other flat teeth. Just a mouthful of canines. A mouth designed for biting.

The creatures shrieked and then the closest one lunged at us. Donny and I turned and fled, scrambling back up the incline. He sobbed and screamed behind me, begging me to hurry. The things shrieked and howled, sounding something like a pack of wild monkeys, and then I heard a scrabbling sound as they raced after us. In my fright, I dropped my phone. Rather than pausing to pick it up, I hurried on.

"There's the light," I yelled to Donny. "I see the daylight!"

I heard Gray, Terry, Cecil and Darnell shouting, but I couldn't understand what they were saying. Then I saw their faces, silhouetted in the sunlight, and their hands reaching for me. Darnell grabbed one of my outstretched wrists and Terry grabbed the other.

"Pull," I pleaded. "Fucking help!"

Behind me, Donny screamed again.

"They've got me! Oh shitarrrhhh . . . "

I rolled on the forest floor, and then jumped to my feet.

"Pull him out," I yelled. "Get him the hell out of there!"

Darnell and Terry had hold of Donny's arms. Cecil crouched in the leaves, staring wide-eyed and in shock. Gray stood to the side, gaping. I rushed over and grabbed hold of Donny's shoulder, and then braced my feet against a rock. All of us strained with the effort. We could feel the creatures trying to yank him back down inside.

Donny lifted his head and shrieked. "They're biting me! My fucking ankles! Help me . . . "

"On three," Terry yelled. "One . . . two . . . "

"Three," I shouted, and we pulled as hard as we could. Donny's back slid into view, and then his waist, and then his legs. I caught a glimpse of two spindly arms with long, thick fingernails clutching Donny's calves. The cuffs of his jeans were ripped and wet with blood. His boots and socks were missing, and the skin on his feet and ankles was shredded. As we yanked him free of the cave, the sunlight glanced across those spindly arms, and the pale skin began to blister and smoke. A howl echoed out of the cave mouth, and the creature let go.

We fell back, dragging Donny into the sun. He wailed and thrashed and ground his teeth. His hands balled up into fists as he clutched the dirt.

"Oh Jesus," Darnell whimpered. "Look at his feet! They're *shredded*! What the hell happened down there?"

They all stared at me in expectant horror. When I opened my mouth to tell them, I threw up all over myself.

Inside the cave, the howls grew louder.

Terry unbuckled his belt and yanked it off. Then he knelt and hurriedly applied a tourniquet to Donny's left foot.

"Darnell," Terry said, "get his other foot."

Donny lay on the ground between them, moaning. His complexion had turned pale and his pupils were dilated. Instead of complying, Darnell stared at the mouth of the cave. The howls coming from inside slowly turned into grunts and snarls.

Darnell turned back to me. "The fuck is that? Where are the others? What the hell happened to you guys down there?"

Cecil's eyes were still wide. "Where's my brother?"

Before I could respond to either of them, Terry reached out and grabbed Darnell's arm.

"Get your belt off and get it around his other foot before he bleeds to death!"

Nodding, Darnell unhooked his belt. His hands shook as he removed it.

"What is it?" Gray asked. "What kind of animal?"

I shook my head. "Not an animal . . . "

"Well, what then?"

"They're . . . I . . . "

Cecil crouched down and grabbed my face in both hands. "Where the hell is Seymour?"

A pair of slender white arms shot out of the cave. Long, yellow fingernails clawed at the dirt and moss. The thing reached for Donny. Shouting, Cecil let go of me and scrambled back, tripping on Terry and sending them both tumbling to the ground. Gray and Darnell scurried out of the way, as well, but Darnell had the presence of mind to grab Donny by the shoulders and haul him clear of the creature's grasp. The thing snarled in frustration.

As the hands and arms emerged further into the sunlight, the skin began to blister and bubble and smoke. It was an instantaneous thing, and the arms quickly retreated, but in that moment, I was reminded of two things from when we were kids. One time, Gray had sprinkled salt on a slug he found crawling on a rock. The effect was horrifying—and yet captivating for a bunch of pre-teen boys. The slug had slowly seemed to dissolve, transforming into a puddle of white froth. Another time, after hearing about it from some older kids, I'd held a magnifying glass over a bustling anthill, stopping only when I saw them begin to smoke and wither. I'd felt horrible about it for weeks after. This was like both of those events. The pale skin sloughed off the arms like wallpaper paste. Blisters popped and oozed like pimples. Smoke curled into the sky. And then the arms were withdrawn, back into the darkness of the cave, leaving only agonized howls and a terrible stench that was like a mix of roadkill and burned hair.

"What the fuck was that?" Darnell yelled. "What the hell is happening?"

Wide-eyed, Terry snatched the belt from Darnell's trembling hands and finished Donny's second tourniquet. Donny reached up and grabbed his shirt.

"Don't let me die," he pleaded.

Terry grabbed his wrist and squeezed. "You're not gonna die."

"P-promise?"

"I promise. We're gonna get you out of here. When we get to some place with cell service, we'll call you an ambulance."

Gray shuffled his feet, but said nothing.

Cecil turned on me again. "Where the hell is Seymour, goddamn it?"

"He's . . . " I swallowed hard.

"Dead?" Cecil whispered.

I nodded. "Him and Mattie both."

He staggered backward, mouth working like a fish out of water. His hands curled into fists at his sides.

Darnell put his hand on my shoulder. "What was that?"

"I . . . I think they're . . . vampires."

He stared at me. Gray and Terry did the same. None of them argued. They'd all seen what had happened to the creature's arms when the sunlight hit them.

"Fuck that," Cecil said, "and fuck you. Vampires my ass!"

"He's r-right," Donny stammered, twitching on the ground. "I s-saw . . . "

Cecil turned toward the cave and dropped to his knees. "Seymour! Seymour, you answer me! Sound off, goddamn it."

"Cecil," Terry said, "look at Donny's feet. Look at the bite marks and—"

"Some kind of animal," Cecil countered. "Seymour, hang on! I'm coming."

"No," I shouted. "You can't—"

He stuck his head and shoulders into the mouth of the cave. For a second, it looked like he was about to crawl the rest of the way in. Then, his entire body stiffened, and he fell belly first to the ground. Cecil let out a garbled, muffled scream that was cut off abruptly. His legs began to jitter, kicking up moss and stones.

"Pull him out," I yelled.

Gray and Terry grabbed hold of Cecil's twitching legs and pulled, grunting with the effort. His body slid back out into the sunlight.

His head stayed inside the cave.

Blood jetted from the mangled stump of his neck, pouring like water spraying from a power washer. Screaming, my cousins let go of Cecil's feet and scurried backward.

The slurping sounds started again, down there in the darkness, loud enough that we heard them over our cries.

"Go," Darnell yelled. "Let's get the fuck out of here!"

"Hang on," Gray said. His voice sounded like he was half asleep. "We've got to get Cecil's head. He'll want it."

"Fuck his head!" Darnell raised his arm and cocked a fist.

I stepped between them. "He's in shock. I reckon we all are. Punching each other ain't gonna help anything."

Terry bent over Donny. "Wrap your arms around my neck, okay?"

Nodding, Donny gritted his teeth and grabbed hold. Terry lifted him up off the ground and turned to me.

"You okay?"

"Yeah," I replied. "Let's just . . . let's go."

Darnell led the way. Terry followed close behind, carrying Donny. I turned back to Gray. He stared down at Cecil's headless corpse. Cecil's legs were still twitching.

"Come on," I urged. "We've got to go."

We ran after the others.

Beneath our feet, the howls started up again.

SEVEN

I DON'T KNOW how long or how far we ran. It could have been a half hour or only a few minutes. We didn't talk to each other so much as just shouted and yelled in general. We were like hunted deer fleeing from a pack of feral dogs, driven by fear and panic rather than any sort of conscious thought. Darnell stayed in the lead, but Terry—slowed down by Donny's weight—soon dropped behind. First, he slipped past me. Then, he fell in behind Gray. I had enough presence of mind not to let our cousin slip completely from our sight, so I slowed my pace. Gray did the same. I don't know if it was a conscious decision on his part, or if he was just following the herd. When Darnell started to get too far ahead, I hollered at him to wait up. He slowed his pace some, but didn't stop completely.

Eventually, we came across a freshwater spring bubbling up out of the ground between two tall pine trees. Even in my numb state of shock, I noticed how lifeless the spot was. It should have been surrounded by flying insects, and home to frogs and salamanders, but there was nothing.

"Wait," Terry panted. "Hold up, boys! I can't go any further."

The three of us stopped and turned. He leaned his back against an oak tree and slowly slid down its length. Then he gently lay Donny on the ground and rested his back, head, and shoulders against the trunk.

"How is he?" I crouched by Donny's side.

"Unconscious," Terry muttered. "I don't know if that's a good thing or a bad thing."

"It's bad," I said.

Donny's complexion had turned as pale as that of the creatures, and there were dark, sunken circles under both his eyes. Worse, his lips had gone from red to gray, like two pieces of chicken liver attached to his face. His chest rose and fell, but slowly. I picked up one limp hand and felt his wrist to check his pulse. His skin was cool and dry.

Darnell knelt down by the spring, cupped some water in his hands, and sipped.

"You're gonna get sick doing that," Gray warned. "There's parasites and shit."

"It's not like I'm drinking from Terry's pond," Darnell said. "It's spring water. Comes up out of the ground. Nothing purer."

"Maybe," I said, "but I reckon there's nothing pure about what's living in the ground beneath this hollow."

Darnell's eyes went wide. He let the rest of the water run through his fingers, and spat.

"Shit! You reckon I'll catch whatever the fuck it is?"

"You'll be fine," Terry said. "But Donny ain't gonna be unless we get him some help."

"His pulse is weak," I said, "and his breathing is shallow."

Terry nodded. "I noticed. Blood loss, I reckon?"

I shrugged. "Maybe. I don't know. Let's get going again. I'll carry him for a bit."

"No." Gray stepped forward. "I'll do it. I got us into this mess. I'll get Donny out."

"Okay," I agreed, "but you give a holler if it gets to be too much. We don't need you having a heart attack on top of everything else."

He stooped over and carefully picked up Donny, who lolled like dead weight in his arms. I reached out and helped Terry to his feet. He grunted in thanks.

"Which way?" Darnell asked.

"I don't fucking know," I said. "We were following you. I figured you knew where you were going."

"Me? I just ran. I didn't think about the direction."

"You didn't think about the . . . " I glanced around. "Well, where the hell are we? I don't remember passing by this spring when we came in! Terry?"

"How should I know?" he asked.

"It's your property, Terry!"

"I told y'all before—I never come here. Nobody does! Far as I know, ain't nobody been in this hollow since our great-grandad."

I looked up at the sky, searching for the sun. It was hard to make out its location through the thick canopy of treetops, and when I did find it, I frowned.

"Is it me," I muttered, "or is the sun further west than it should be?"

The others craned their heads, and looked.

"Well, I'll be dipped in shit," Gray said. "It is. Reckon we've been in here longer than we thought."

"Which means it's that much closer to sundown," I said. "We've got to go, boys!"

"This way, I think." Terry pointed. "If that's west, then this is north. Should bring us out yonder near the truck."

He took the lead. Darnell and I followed him. Gray came last, carrying Donny.

"What happens at sundown?" Darnell asked.

I turned to him. "Vampires can only come out after dark, right?"

"Wait, you were serious about that?"

"Well, yeah. You got a better explanation?"

"No, but vampires? I mean . . . I thought that was just something you said in the moment, you know?"

"You didn't see them. Donny and I did. I can't think of a better word for them. And besides, y'all saw what they did to Donny's feet. And what they did to Cecil? They did the same to Seymour and Mattie. And the one that tried to crawl out of the cave—you saw what happened when the sunlight hit it. If those aren't vampires, then I don't know what is."

"I drank the water," Darnell yelled. "Am I gonna turn into a vampire?"

"You don't turn into a vampire from drinking water," I said.

"How do you know, Frank? It's like you said, they live underground, which is where the water came from. What if I'm infected?"

"They're not vampires," Terry argued.

"You got a better explanation?" I asked.

"Okay," Terry said, "let's say they're vampires. How'd they stay alive so long?"

A twig snapped under my boot. "What do you mean?"

"They've got to eat, same as everyone else, right?

Well, what have they been eating? If they were sneaking out of this hollow come nightfall, then me and my family would have been sucked dry long ago. I reckon the rest of this county would have followed."

"Maybe they're eating animals," I suggested.

"That's possible," Terry said, "but other than that dead bear and those dead coyotes, we haven't seen a single living thing in this hollow the whole time we've been here. If they are vampires, then they've got to be starved."

"Yeah," I agreed. "I think they are. You didn't see them. They were . . . scrawny looking things. Emaciated. You ever see those photos from the Nazi concentration camps?"

Terry nodded.

"That's what they looked like," I said. "Just skin and bones."

His complexion paled. "Good Lord . . . "

"All the more reason for us to get the hell out of here, then," Darnell said.

Gray huffed behind us. I stopped and turned.

"You okay? Want me to take him for a bit?"

"No," he panted. "I've got him. Just hard to talk and carry him at the same time."

I turned around and we kept going. After a few minutes, we came to a fallen tree, leaning against a still-standing tree. Terry stopped and turned his head left to right. Then he pulled out his tobacco, packed it quickly, and stuffed a plug between his lip and gum.

"Yeah," he said. "I'm pretty sure this is the right direction. Come on."

"Donny was bit, right?" Darnell asked.

"Yeah," I replied. "You saw it."

"Okay, well, let's say you're right. Let's say that whatever was in that cave is really a pack of vampires—if they bit him, then doesn't that mean he'd turn into one next?"

Behind us, Donny groaned and stirred.

"Oh Jesus," Gray moaned.

He was so startled that he stumbled and dropped Donny, who fell to the forest floor like a rock. Gray yelped, mortified by what he'd done. Donny, however, didn't cry out. He simply lay there on his back, grinding his teeth and slowly wriggling his legs and arms, fingers clawing at the leaves and dirt, head twisting back and forth as he gazed up at us, wide-eyed.

"For fuck's sake, Gray," Darnell yelled. "Watch what you're doing!"

"I didn't mean to drop him! He just surprised me."

We all rushed over to Donny and knelt by his side. When I reached out and gently touched his cheek, I noticed that his skin was cold.

"Hey," I said. "How are you doing, buddy? You holding up okay?"

Donny tried to speak, but all that came out was a dry croak. He licked his gray, cracked lips, and I saw that his tongue had turned as ashen-colored as the rest of him.

"Don't try to move," Darnell told him. "Just lay still. We're gonna get you some help."

"Cecil," Donny rasped, looking around. "Seymour? Mattie?"

"They're dead," Terry told him. "They're dead, buddy."

"Don't you remember?" Gray asked.

"Hungry," Donny whispered. "That's all I know. I'm hungry."

"We'll get you something to eat soon as we make it out of the hollow," I said. I motioned at the tourniquets around his ankles. "Should we loosen those for a minute? Anybody know?"

"I'm not sure," Terry replied, "but he's awfully pale."

"Let's see." I slowly unfastened one of the belts. The ragged gashes in Donny's ankle had stopped bleeding. Frowning, I fastened the tourniquet around him again and cinched it up.

"That's not normal," I said.

"What?" Gray asked.

"He's stopped bleeding."

"What?" Terry and Darnell chimed in.

"Check for yourselves."

"I . . . see them." Donny dug his fingers into the soil. Dry leaves crunched and tiny twigs snapped in his grasp. "I can see them, boys."

"He's delirious," Terry said.

Darnell nodded. "I reckon he's in shock. Feel how cold he is? We need a blanket or something."

Terry unbuttoned and shrugged off his long sleeve flannel shirt, revealing a faded black Dale Earnhardt t-shirt beneath it. He draped the flannel over Donny's chest and abdomen.

"There ya go, buddy. That will keep you warm."

"I can hear . . . them . . . "

"It's okay, Donny." I did my best to sound reassuring. "They're not here. We're nowhere near the cave. It's going to be okay."

He shook his head and grinned. It was a terrible,

unsettling expression. Then, he slowly moved his arm. It looked like it pained him to do so. He extended his index finger and tapped the side of his head.

"In here. I . . . can hear and see them . . . "

"Come on, y'all." Darnell stood up. "He's gonna die right here if we don't get moving. Terry, you gotta take the lead."

"Why me?"

"Because it's your property, motherfucker!"

"Don't call me a motherfucker, Darnell! None of this shit is my fault. There's no need for that kind of talk."

Ignoring them, I met Donny's frightened gaze. Then, I picked up his hand and squeezed.

"I'm . . . so . . . c-cold . . . "

"You've got to hang on, okay?"

He grunted.

"Just hold on. We'll get you out of here."

"H-hungry . . . it hurts . . . "

Frowning, I held his hand a minute longer. Slowly, I slid my grasp down to his wrist.

Donny had no pulse.

It was all I could do to keep my expression neutral. I didn't want Donny to see how alarmed I was. I tried to smile, and gently lay his hand down beside him. Then I stood up. Darnell had just come over to pick him up, but I put a hand on his chest and shook my head.

"What's wrong?" he asked.

I nodded my head to my left, and walked out of Donny's line of sight. Darnell, Gray and Terry followed.

"What is it?" Darnell asked.

"He's dead."

All three of them glanced at Donny and then back to me.

"No he's not," Terry said. "He's over there moving around right now."

"I see that," I agreed, "but I'm tellin' y'all, he ain't got a pulse."

"It was probably just weak," Gray said. "He's lost a lot of blood, after all."

"Check him yourself," I said.

"What the fuck are we standing around here arguing about this for?" Darnell shook his head. "Obviously, he ain't dead. But he's gonna be if we don't get a move on, goddamn it."

He turned back to Donny, and squared his shoulders.

"Wait." I reached for him.

Darnell pulled away, shrugging me off. Then he stomped back over to where Donny lay, bent down, and carefully picked him up.

"Damn, Donny," he grunted. "If I didn't know better, I'd say you lost weight. You're light as a feather."

"He wasn't before," Gray said.

"How's that?" Terry asked.

"He wasn't light when I was carrying him."

"You're just out of shape," Darnell said.

"Fuck you," Gray countered. "Terry, lead us out of here before I punch him?"

Nodding, Terry took a deep breath and glanced around, trying to get his bearings. Darnell walked back over to us, cradling Donny in his arms.

"Which way?" Darnell asked.

"I'm . . . hungry," Donny whined.

"I know, buddy." Darnell looked down at him and smiled. His voice was choked with emotion. "Listen. When we get out of here, I'm going to take you to Biscuit World, and you can eat your way through the whole damn menu."

Grinning, Donny drooled. I took that as a good sign. His mouth had been so dry before. I stood there, lost in thought. Obviously, I'd been wrong about his pulse.

"We'll all go to Biscuit World," Terry agreed.

"Now I'm hungry, too," Gray said.

Donny weakly raised his arm, and touched Darnell's cheek. His mouth moved, but none of us could hear him.

"What's that, Donny?" Darnell lowered his head.

Donny lunged in his arms, biting at his neck.

Darnell let out a strangled sort of scream and flung Donny away from him. For the second time in just a few minutes, Donny fell to the forest floor, landing in a tangle of bushes.

This time, however, he didn't lay sprawled there, twitching and moaning. Instead, he rolled over and scurried to his feet, adopting a crouched, defensive stance. He stayed there, in the deep shade of some thick-leaved overhanging tree branches. His eyes darted back and forth between each of us. His lips curled back from his clenched teeth, revealing long incisors that hadn't been there before. He hissed, sounding more like those things in the cave than he did the guy we'd grown up with.

"He fucking bit me!"

I hurried toward Darnell. "Let me see."

He had one hand clamped over his neck. He waved me away with his other hand. "Get the fuck back."

"Bullshit, Darnell. Let me fucking see it!"

I rushed him, and forced his hand away from his neck. The skin wasn't broken, but there was ugly bruising from where Donny had tried to bite him.

"Oh, Jesus," Darnell whined. "How bad is it? Did he get my jugular?"

"Relax." I gripped his shoulder hard. "You're not bleeding. You're fine."

"He fucking bit me! Now I'm gonna be a vampire, for sure."

"He didn't break the skin! Calm down. You're okay."

Moaning, Darnell stumbled backward into a tree and slumped to his haunches. "Ah, God. Oh, fuck . . . "

Donny hissed again. I whipped around, expecting him to spring at me. Instead, he stayed where he was, in the shade. I side-stepped and ran over to Terry and Gray. Donny watched me, his hands outstretched, teeth still bared.

"I'm hungry," he said. "Come on fellas. Help me out."

"You s-stay the hell back," Terry stammered.

Donny turned to Darnell. His tone became softer and apologetic. "I'm sorry, man. I didn't mean to freak you out."

"Freak me out? Motherfucker, you tried to bite my neck open!"

"Yeah, but I didn't mean to. It was just . . . I couldn't control myself."

"Donny . . . " I held up my hands and took one tentative step toward him. "You're not yourself. You know that, right?"

He stared at me for a moment. Then his expression crumbled, and he began to cry. His body shook, and while his sorrow seemed to be real, I noticed that no actual tears were coming from his eyes.

"I know," he sobbed. "I'm sorry, guys. I really am. My head is all fucked up right now."

"Talk to us," I said. "Tell us what's going on."

"I could smell Darnell's blood." He sighed. "You know like when you field dress a deer—that first smell of blood after you cut in with your knife? It was like that, but . . . richer. Bolder."

"My blood ain't a cup of fucking coffee, Donny!"

"I know, but I wanted it just like a person wants a cup of coffee. I could hear it flowing in your veins. I can hear all kinds of things now. Stuff y'all could never hear."

As he talked, Donny dropped his menacing stance, but he didn't entirely relax. I noticed that he was careful to stay in the deep shade, and not step out into the sunlight. When I glanced at my cousins, I was pretty sure that Gray had picked up on that, as well. It was there in his careful expression. Terry, on the other hand, just looked horrified.

Something else I noticed was that his ankles no longer seemed to be injured. They'd been torn to shreds and we'd had to carry him, but now he was moving around just fine.

"Like what?" Gray asked. "What can you hear, Donny?"

"Birds, and the beat of a butterfly's wings, way over yonder, beyond the hollow. They're in Terry's pasture right now. They don't come in here. They know better. Anything that comes in here ends up eaten. It's like the bear and those coyotes. The bear was sick when it wandered in. They ate it."

"Who ate it?" I asked.

He smiled, sadly. "You know who. And after they drained it, they left the carcass to lie there as bait. When the coyotes smelled it, and came slinking in, they ate them, too. But that's the thing, boys. Most animals know better than to come in this hollow. So, they have to wait for the occasional squirrel or bird or bug, and they're so goddamned hungry. They're hungry all the time, and they're weak. Nothing like what they should be."

"Donny," I asked, "how do you know all this?"

He shrugged. "It's in my head. I'm one of them now. I know things, instinctively. It's like I can see this whole hidden history in my head. I don't understand a lot of it, but it's there all the same."

"He's fucking crazy." Darnell gave Donny a wide berth as he circled back around to us.

"Everybody just shut up for a minute." Gray pulled out a pack of smokes, tapped one out, and stuck it in his mouth. He patted his pockets, and then frowned. "Shit, My lighter is still in the damn cave."

"That's your number one concern right now?" I asked.

Ignoring me, Gray turned to Donny. "Listen now, Donny. Come over here and let us get you to a hospital."

Donny snorted. "You want me to come out in the

sunlight, Gray? Is that it? Want me to burn up like the one back at the cave did?"

"No, I just want to get you some help."

"There ain't no help for what I've become. And you boys better leave here while you still can."

"You're not a goddamned vampire," Terry yelled. "Something happened to you, yes. But it ain't that. If you were a vampire, then how come Seymour, Cecil, and Mattie didn't turn into vampires, too?"

"Because there's nothing left of them," Donny explained. "I was bitten. They were drained. The others—the ones down in the cave—they fed well for the first time in a long time. But that means they'll be faster now. Stronger. Hungrier."

"Like the Six Million Dollar Man," Darnell muttered.

"You ain't funny," Terry said, and then turned back to Donny. "Okay, let's say all of that is true, Donny. Then how come these things ain't ever showed up at my house? How come there's not vampires all over Greenbrier County?"

"The garlic," Donny replied, licking his lips. "Ask your great-grandfather. He knew."

"And he's dead," I said, "so it's a little hard to ask him."

"The garlic . . . there's something about it. Something toxic. It kills us just as sure as sunlight does. At one point in time, there were just a few wild patches of it, and they could come and go. But back around the early nineteen hundreds, it began to spread, and they got trapped in here. Even in winter time, they can't leave, because of the roots and the bulbs underground."

"That don't make sense," Terry said.

"Oh?" Darnell said. "That's the thing about all of this that doesn't make sense to you? The garlic?"

Donny snarled suddenly, and dropped to the ground, holding himself upright with one hand. He whipped his head from side to side, and long lines of drool dribbled from his mouth.

"You guys have to go," he gasped. "And you've gotta go now! The sun is sinking fast."

Gray glanced at his watch. "We've got at least another hour before it's dark."

"It doesn't have to be full dark," Donny explained. "Not here in the hollow. It gets darker here quicker than it does out there. They'll be coming for you, and my God, they're fast. I'll try . . . I'll try not to. I'm sorry again, Darnell."

"Donny . . . " Terry stepped toward him.

Gray reached out, grabbed his shoulder, and shook his head. "Don't go near him."

"Bullshit—"

"Listen to him," Donny said. "I ain't your friend no more, Terry. Like I said, I'm going to try not to, but I can't promise anything. Y'all smell so good. Your blood, inside you, all warm and salty . . . "

He made a trilling sound in the back of his throat.

I glanced up at the sky. It was definitely getting darker.

"Come on," I said.

We ran.

Behind us, Donny howled.

EIGHT

"WHICH WAY?" Gray panted.

"Follow Terry," I yelled.

Terry responded with a mournful whimper.

We fled, stumbling over roots and scrambling up embankments. Terry was in the lead, followed closely by myself and then Gray. Darnell ran beside me, still holding his neck.

Tree limbs lashed my face like whips, and thorns and vines gripped my pants and shirt. I tore free, heedless of the pain or damage to my clothing. Indeed, I barely noticed anything at all. I focused only on my cousin's back, trying hard to keep up with him and praying that he knew where he was going. My breath began to burn in my chest, and then my pulse started pounding loud in my temples. My left arm tingled. I didn't know if it was just fear, or if I was about to have a heart attack or a stroke. Regardless, I pushed on, terrified of the idea of being incapacitated there in the hollow, helpless prey for those creatures.

And for Donny, too.

It seemed impossible. I'm not talking about the vampires. Obviously, they had seemed impossible at first, as well. But I had an easier time accepting their reality than I did the fact that my friend – a guy I'd known since we were kids – was now one of them, and possibly hunting us at that moment. Equally impossible was the fact that Mattie, Cecil and Seymour were all dead. That didn't feel real. Part of me kept expecting to hear them call out for help, or come charging out of the woods to flee with us. I had a sudden, bizarre urge to go back and check on them. I knew it was silly. I'd seen their corpses. Hell, Cecil didn't have a head anymore. There was no way he could have lived through that. But the urge was there, all the same. These were guys I had grown up with, shared a life with—fishing together in the Greenbrier River and down at the old catfish hole, riding four-wheelers all over the backwoods and hills, summers spent camping out for days in the State Forest, hunting deer and turkeys and bears together, poker and video game nights, trips up to Morgantown to see the Mountaineers play, evenings spent hanging out in Terry's backyard, arguing music and politics and everything else friends argue about, reliving our glory days and making new glory days, as well. How could they be gone? How could all of that just be over? It had all happened so suddenly. That morning, we'd all been together over at Terry's house. We'd all come into this hollow together. It didn't seem right that we were leaving without them.

"It's getting darker," Gray gasped, breathless. "It's still early, though. It ain't natural."

"It's natural," I argued. "We're in a thick hollow. Of course it's going to get darker here first. Donny was right about that. Just stay focused."

We came to a small shale bank, and Darnell finally

let go of his neck, and started to clamber up the side. Slivers of rock slid down behind him. I noticed some little white fossils—ferns and such. Any other time, I'd have been fascinated by them. It occurred to me that Seymour would have been, too, had he lived long enough to see them.

"Come on," Darnell urged. "Move your asses."

"Not that way." Terry pointed to our left. "We have to go around and head yonder."

"Bullshit! Your truck is up that way."

"No, it's not," Terry argued. "I remember this shale bank being to our right when we came in."

Darnell glanced at me and Gray.

I shrugged. "I didn't notice it before."

"Me either," Gray said.

"Fuck it," Darnell said. "I'm going this way."

He resumed his climb. More shale slipped down behind him. He grabbed at a fern for support, and it yanked free of the embankment, roots and all. Darnell slid back down.

"Shit."

He frantically tried to climb again, and I realized that it was panic that was determining his actions.

"Darnell," I spoke calmly, "Terry says to go this way. I'm inclined to listen to him."

Gray nodded. "Yep. Ain't no sense in splitting up. We've got to—"

Darnell whirled around. "Fuck you, Gray! This whole thing is your fucking fault to begin with. You had to go and get mixed up in some bullshit with the Russian mob, and you roped us into it, and now Cecil and Seymour and Mattie are dead, and Donny—"

"I didn't put a gun to your head," Gray argued.

"You came of your own free will, Darnell. All of you did!"

"So that makes it okay, then?"

"That's not what I said! What I'm saying is that we all need to stick together."

Darnell sneered. "Yeah, because that's worked out so well up till now. These are fucking vampires, boys. Okay? I believe. You happy? We're dealing with goddamn vampires. Now, I don't know about the rest of you, but I've seen enough horror movies to know what happens to the black guy. That ain't gonna be me."

I held up a hand. "Darnell—"

"No," he yelled. "I'm done listening and I'm done arguing. I'm getting the hell out of here, and I'm going this way. If you're coming, then come on. If not, then I'll meet up with y'all out by the truck, if you make it. And Gray?"

"Yeah?"

"I'm gonna beat your ass when I see you there."

"I'm sorry, Darnell."

Gray's tone was one of utter defeat, but Darnell didn't seem to care.

"Fuck you and your apologies. I'll catch y'all later."

"Darnell . . . " I started forward, reaching for him.

He turned away from us and began climbing again, sending more pieces of shale sliding down behind him. This time, he made it to the top. I thought maybe he would pause and glance back down at us, but he didn't. Instead, Darnell slipped through a tangle of underbrush and then disappeared from sight.

The shadows around us deepened.

"Come on," Terry said. "There's not much light left. We've got to hurry."

He hurried off in the direction he had indicated earlier. Gray quickly followed after him. I stood there for a moment, staring up at the top of the shale bank, debating whether to go with Darnell, or stick with my cousins. Terry and Gray's forms grew dim as the gloom deepened. It almost seemed to me as if the darkness was seeping up out of the ground.

"Shit . . . "

Shoulders slumping, I hurried along after my cousins.

Blood is thicker than water, they say.

But it flows like water. I can tell you that.

NINE

ONE SUMMER, back when we were kids, Gray, Terry and I were walking along a dirt road just off the old McCullum farm. That place had been long abandoned even back then. I doubt there's much of anything left standing there today. If I remember correctly, Mattie had tried to scavenge there a few years back, and said there wasn't much left.

Even back then, though, nature had been starting to reclaim that dirt road due to disuse. It was rutted with ditches and potholes from storm runoff, and choked with tall weeds and wildflowers, and at one spot, a shallow creek ran across it. We'd stopped at that creek to look for crayfish, when Terry had noticed something just on the other side, lying motionless in the sun. It was a big, black snake—the largest any of us had ever seen at that point in our lives. Thick as a gearshift knob and long enough that the head and the tail were both obscured by the weeds. It was a good ten or fifteen feet away. All we could see was the body, sunning itself.

To this day, I don't know why he did it, but Gray reached down, picked a flat rock out of the stream—the kind of stone that's perfect for skipping across the water's surface—and threw it at the snake. The rock struck its side and glanced off. Far as we could tell, the snake wasn't injured. But boy, was it pissed off! That thing's head and tail whipped around, and it glared at us for one brief moment, and then it charged, slithering across that water and closing the distance between us in just a few seconds. We'd never seen anything move so fast. We turned and ran, all three of us screaming bloody murder, and the snake gave chase. I remember I was in the rear, and I was crying, because at any minute, I expected to feel its fangs rip into my ankle, or to feel it wrap itself around my leg. I didn't dare risk a glance behind me, because if I saw it chasing us, I might have collapsed from fright.

That snake pursued us a good quarter of a mile or so before finally dropping back. We ran at least a full mile before stopping.

I thought of the snake when the vampires appeared. They moved just as fast. One minute, we were scrambling through the gloom, panicked and breathless and urging each other on. Terry hesitated for just a moment, trying to get his bearings.

The sun finished its descent.

Terry glanced back at us and pointed ahead to the right. "I think we need to—"

He never finished. There was a blur of movement from both sides, and then two of the creatures from the cave were upon him. I don't know where they came from. One minute there was nothing. The next, they were there. Our younger cousin never stood a chance. They fell on him, growling and hissing, seizing his arms and pulling. Terry let out a high-pitched wail. He thrashed, trying to break free. Then they wrenched his arms from their sockets with a terrible popping sound. Terry's eyes went wide, and his mouth twisted in agony. Blood jetted from both sockets, splashing his face, and the surrounding vegetation, and me and Gray.

Shrieking, I stumbled backward as another blur rocketed toward us from the left. It looked sort of like billowing steam or smoke being pushed ahead by a gust of wind. Then it solidified next to Gray and lunged for his neck. Gray flung himself to the ground at the last moment, and the vampire stumbled past him.

Terry sank to his knees, still spraying blood. It shot out of him like water from a garden hose. Worse than that, though, was his expression—a look of knowing, helpless horror. His attackers knelt beside him and—expectant mouths open wide—buried their faces in his empty, gushing arm sockets. They made terrible lapping and gulping sounds as they gorged themselves.

Donny had been right when he talked about them feeding. It was hard for me to believe that these were the same scrawny creatures we had found in the cave earlier. They were thicker now. More robust. Their eyes were no longer dull and listless, and their lips had lost that gray color. With each one of us they killed, they grew stronger. They'd been starving, feeding on the occasional animal unlucky enough to wander into this hollow. They'd waited in that weakened state for God knows how long. And then we'd come along, a willing party to Gray's stupid idea—a walking, talking smorgasbord. Now . . . they were ravenous. Frenzied.

The third vampire spun around and lunged at Gray, who had snatched up a dead tree branch from the ground and was holding it up in front of him, yelling incoherently. Too late, the bloodsucker fell on the makeshift weapon. The wood pierced its abdomen. The vampire wailed. Screaming, Gray shoved the length deeper. His attacker reeled backward, fangs bared, and pulled itself free. Blood trickled from the wound, along with a thicker, darker fluid. I had an inkling that the latter was what flowed through the vampire's veins, and the blood itself was what it had sucked out of our friends but hadn't fully digested yet.

Enraged, the vampire made a grab at Gray, but he scurried backward, thrusting the branch in front of him like a spear.

"Get back," he yelled. "Stay the hell back, you fucking thing!"

I hesitated, frozen with fear and panic. I glanced over at Terry and saw that he was looking at me with a mournful expression on his face. He knew what was happening to him. He understood. His attackers had forced him onto his back, and as he lay there on the forest floor, they burrowed their faces deeper into his wounds. Terry mouthed something at me, but I couldn't tell what it was. Then he repeated it again.

"Tell my mother that I . . . "

His mother—my aunt Lena—had been dead for four years.

A moment later, Terry was dead, too.

He took a deep, shuddering breath and seemed to hold it. His eyes were still focused on me, but as I watched, they glazed over. If he breathed out again, I never heard it.

Gray shrieked. I turned back to him and saw that the vampire had gotten around his weapon, and had latched itself onto his face. Its jaws were stretched impossibly wide, and its mouth was pressed tightly over his left eye socket. The creature's cheeks fluttered. Gray kicked and flailed. There was a sucking sound, and then a muffled pop, and Gray stiffened like he'd been shocked. The vampire clutched his head in its hands and fed greedily. I couldn't see the hole in its belly, given the monster's position, but that injury hadn't seemed to dampen its appetite any.

I fled. I'm not proud of it. I didn't think about it. I was operating purely on instinct. I forgot all about my cousins and all about Darnell, still wandering around out there somewhere, and I ran in the direction Terry had pointed us toward just a few minutes before. I cried and screamed, babbling nonsensically, barely noticing as once again, thorns and branches whipped and tore at me as I barreled on.

I tripped over a root in the dark and went sprawling onto the forest floor, knocking the wind from my lungs and cutting my palms open. I sobbed, expecting the vampires to leap on me, but death didn't come.

Shuddering, I stumbled to my feet and risked a glance behind me. It was too dark to see where I'd come from, but I could hear them feasting.

I decided not to wait around and become dessert, so I took a deep breath and kept running. I don't know how long that was. It seemed like forever, but it was probably only a few minutes. The thought occurred to me that maybe I should try climbing a tree, but I reckoned the vampires could reach me just as easy there.

The undergrowth began to thin, and the trees spread out. I glimpsed stars above me, and a glimmer of moonlight. I knew that meant I was approaching the clearing. I lowered my head, squared my shoulders, and pushed on, focusing on the tree line. The vegetation thinned even more, and I spotted the field through the trees. It was about half a football field away. I poured it on then, praying as I ran, beseeching a God that I didn't even believe in, that if He would help me get out of here alive, I'd do whatever He wanted.

The ground sloped upward, and I scrambled along in a loping sort of stride, using my hands to help propel me. I pushed past a boulder and skidded to a halt.

There, in front of me, seated on a fallen log, was Donny. He held Darnell in his arms, gently, like a lover. But Darnell wasn't moving, and there was something off about him. He looked skinnier than normal, as if he'd lost a shocking amount of weight. His skin hung off his body in wrinkled sags, and his eyes and cheeks looked sunken. After a moment, I realized why.

He'd been drained of blood.

And Donny, always too-thin from living off welfare checks and whatever he could grow or shoot, looked positively swollen.

He looked up at me and grinned, flashing a new pair of ivory white fangs. Then he licked his lips. The corners of his mouth were crusted with Darnell's blood. His shredded ankles had completely healed. He looked healthier than he had in years.

"Howdy," he said. "What took you so long?"

"Donny . . . " My voice cracked with horror and grief. "What did you do?"

His grin faltered, and then faded. He glanced down at Darnell's limp form, and for a moment, his expression turned to sadness.

"I know," he said. "I know. Reckon I just couldn't stop myself."

"Is he . . . ?"

"Dead?"

I nodded.

The smile flickered on his face again, and then receded. "What you really mean is, dead like Mattie and Cecil and Seymour or is he dead like me?"

I shrugged, unable to speak around the lump in my throat, afraid that if I opened my mouth, I'd start screaming and never stop.

"He's *dead* dead," Donny confirmed. "I won't lie to you. I thought about making him like me. It's an easy thing to do. The way it works is you don't drain the body. You just give them a little bite and drink just a little bit. And I thought about it, because I don't mean you fellas no harm."

"How do you know?"

He tapped his head with his index finger. "Comes with the transformation, I guess."

I shook my head.

"Don't be mad," he pleaded. "You're my friends. All of you. You're the best goddamned friends I've ever had."

"But that didn't stop you from killing Darnell, did it?"

"No, it didn't. When I come across Darnell, his heart was beating so fast, and I could hear it. I mean, just loud as day, like gunshots popping off. And, well . . . I don't know. Something took over inside of me. I heard that heart pounding and I smelled his blood pumping through his veins, and . . . " He sighed, shuddering, and glanced down again at Darnell's corpse. "I just couldn't help myself."

"You killed him. Darnell ain't never done a bad thing to you, Donny, and you fucking killed him like a rabbit!"

He nodded. "Yeah. I did. Ain't no denying it. Reckon that's something I'll have to live with the rest of my life. And from what I can tell, that's forever, less somebody shoves a wooden stake through my heart or drags me out into the sunlight or poisons me with garlic."

"So, that stuff works?"

As I spoke, I slowly started to edge my way around him, shuffling closer to the edge of the hollow. If Donny noticed, he gave no indication.

"Sure." He nodded. "That stuff works. That's about the only things that work. The rest of it is just Hollywood bullshit, made up by folks who don't know their ass from a hole in the ground. But garlic and sunlight and piercing my heart with wood will do the trick. That's why they didn't slaughter me, the way they did the others. Remember? I ate the garlic? They got a taste of it when they bit into my legs. That's why they let me go. And that's why I'm one of them no, instead of just getting slaughtered like the others."

"What about crosses? Or running water?"

"They don't do shit. And before you ask, I can't turn into a bat, either. Or . . . if I can, then I don't know how."

I took another sideways step. When Donny didn't react, I decided to keep him talking.

"Earlier, Gray stabbed one of the others with a tree branch. Right through the abdomen. But that didn't kill the vampire. Why not? Does it have to be an actual wooden stake or something?"

"Nah." He waved one hand dismissively. "I reckon a tree branch works just as good as a any other length of wood. At least, as far as I can tell. A lot of this stuff is still knew to me, remember."

"Then, why didn't it work?"

"Gray probably didn't hit the heart. That's the key. Did the vampire bleed?"

"No," I replied. "Not really. I mean, there was blood, but I think most of that belonged to Mattie, Seymour and Cecil. And there was some black stuff, that wasn't blood."

"The black stuff is what we've got inside of us. See, our hearts don't beat. Not like yours. We've got no pulse, so there's nothing to move the blood around in our veins. But the black stuff is there instead. It's what keeps us . . . alive. What keeps us vampires."

"What is it?"

He shrugged. "Your guess is as good as mine."

"I thought you knew everything now?"

"Yeah, but I don't know what it's made of or how it works. I never took chemistry when we were in school. Come to think of it, neither did you."

Despite the situation, I grinned. "Yeah. We had Mr. Crenshaw's bonehead math class. Remember, that's what they used to call it? Math for kids who weren't going off to college."

"Which was most of us," Donny agreed. Then he

sighed again. The sound was wistful. "Damn, I miss those days. I often look back on them. I mean, even despite the fact that I flunked out and they wouldn't let me graduate, I reckon that was when my life was best. You guys went on and had families and such, but for me? High school was it. That was the high point."

"It doesn't have to be. You could still . . . "

I stopped, realizing the futility of what I was saying.

"I could still what? Make a life for myself?" Donny sneered derisively and glanced into the woods. Then he turned back to me. His expression was serious. "I don't reckon that's true. I'm trapped here now, just like them."

"I'm sorry," I said, and I meant it.

He was quiet for a moment. Then he smiled.

"I see you trying to sneak away, Frank. I'm not dumb. And I want you to know that I'm resisting it."

"Resisting what? The urge to fucking eat me?"

"Sure." He nodded. "That, too. I can hear your heart, same as Darnell's, and I can smell your blood. But that ain't it. Mostly, I'm resisting the urge to make you like me. I can't leave this place. Not with all that wild garlic growing around the edges of the hollow. You're gonna take off, and the rest of our friends are dead, and that just leaves me. Me and them other vampires. They're strangers. I don't want to be alone here with them. Forever is a long time to be lonely."

"I . . . "

"Run." He stirred. Darnell slipped from his lap and flopped onto the forest floor. "I mean it, Frank. Get out of here while you still can. I don't think I can hold off much longer."

"Fight it," I urged. "Maybe we can still get you some help. There's got to be somebody in the world that knows about this stuff."

Donny stood up. "There's no help for me. I don't want help. The only thing I want is to not be left alone here."

"Alicia," I reminded him. "She needs me. Yeah, she's going off to college, but a girl still needs her daddy. Please . . . "

"That's what I'm saying. It ain't fair of me to take you from her." Donny's voice grew louder. "But you don't understand how good your blood smells. I can't fight it much longer. Now, run, goddamn it!"

"I'm sorry, Donny."

"I'm sorry, too."

I turned and fled, heading toward the tree line and the field beyond. It drew closer and closer, until there was more moonlight than darkness, and more open space than closed-in vegetation. I was crying so hard that my vision grew hazy through my tears, and everything began to blur. I stumbled, nearly running into a tree, and as I swerved, I heard something rustling behind me.

Donny laughed wildly as he launched himself through the air at me. He slammed into me like a football tackle, pummeling me to the ground. His teeth flashed in the moonlight, white and sharp and glistening. I shoved one palm beneath his chin and shoved his head aloft, keeping it away from my neck, but doing so was an effort. He was strong—much stronger than he'd ever been in life. He moaned and grunted unintelligibly, sounding more like a wild animal than anything else. My fingertips slid across his curled lips and those horrible teeth, and I shuddered, repulsed.

My free hand closed around a fallen stick. Donny pinned my other arm to the ground with his grip, but I snatched the stick up in my free hand and with a yell, I plunged it into his neck, just beneath his chin. Darnell's blood gushed out of Donny's wound, splattering my face. I closed my eyes and mouth and turned away, sputtering. Then I shoved the stick harder and higher, feeling it punch through his tongue and into the roof of his mouth. Donny thrashed and squealed. His eyes rolled around, and then focused on me. The rage I saw reflected there was unlike anything I'd ever seen him express when he was alive. Snapping his mouth shut, he wrenched free of my grip and sat up. The stick jutted from beneath his chin. Donny fumbled at it with his dirty fingers, but the wood was so slick with Darnell's blood, that he had difficulty grasping it.

I turned and scampered forward on my hands and knees, clearing the tree line. I clawed at the dirt in the field, desperately pulling myself forward. Donny howled behind me, but I didn't dare turn around. The fact that he was able to make that sound told me that he'd pulled the stake free. Just as my knees cleared the hollow and I was about to clamber to my feet, something slashed at my ankle. I lashed out, kicking Donny square in the face. He squawked and let loose. I jumped up and ran. Screeching with rage, he gave chase. But when I passed the wild garlic, I jogged to a stop and turned around to look at him. He slid to a halt, and then doubled over and retched. He held his hands out in front of him, as if to ward the garlic off. Then, slowly, he raised his head to face me.

I bent over, hands on my hips, gasping for breath. I tried to speak, but I didn't have the wind for it.

Donny tried to speak, as well, but I'd done so much damage to his mouth, that what he said was garbled and unintelligible. I like to think that maybe it was an apology, but deep down inside, I reckon it was something else entirely.

We stood there staring at one another. After a moment, he took one faltering step forward, and then the garlic affected him again. Reeling, Donny fell back, retreating into the hollow.

He turned back to me one last time. My last memory of him was his pale white face, silhouetted there in the darkness beyond those trees. His expression was mournful. Then it was gone, as if someone had flicked off a light switch.

I collapsed to my knees in the field, and I wept.

Then I screamed.

When the tears and the screams had subsided and I had no more of either left in me, I stumbled across the field and eventually made my way back to Terry's truck. He'd left it unlocked. I flung open the door and wearily sank into the passenger seat. Then I popped the glove compartment and rooted around inside until I found the first aid kit he kept in there for when we went hunting. I fumbled it open and doctored the cuts on my ankle, spraying them with disinfectant and bandaging them as best I could.

I sat there for a long time, unsure of what to do next.

Eventually, I hiked over the hills and returned to

my own truck, still parked there in Terry's driveway, along with everyone else's vehicles—including Darnell's neighbor's shitty Dodge. It didn't seem possible that we'd all been laughing about that earlier and now Darnell was dead.

There were no lights on in Terry's house. His wife and kids must have been asleep. Given that Terry had been out with his cousins and his friends, they probably had assumed he'd be home late, and wouldn't notice anything was amiss until morning. I thought about knocking on the door, and calling the police, but I was exhausted and heartsick and in a considerable amount of shock.

Instead, I started my truck and drove home on those dark, winding country roads. I don't remember much of it. I was pretty much operating on instinct by then. I know I cried some more, but I don't think I screamed. That part was done.

When I got home, I stumbled to my bedroom, collapsed onto the mattress, and slept like the dead.

TEN

S O . . . THAT'S THE STORY. That's what happened. And before you say anything else, let me just state, for the record and such, that I don't give a shit if you don't believe me or not. I know what happened. I know what I'm talking about, and like I said before, here are the things you need to know about vampires.

First of all, we don't dress in black. We're not high-cultured, well-mannered, nicely groomed or perfectly fucking coiffed. I mean, I reckon there might be some like that, elsewhere in the world, but not around these parts. Vampires don't form secret societies and war with other creatures of the night. We don't hang out in cemeteries and tombs, listening to Bauhaus and Type O Negative and smoking clove cigarettes and whining about how much eternal life sucks. Vampires don't have existential crises, because vampires barely have any thoughts beyond what's for dinner. We don't feel love or angst—at least, not the way you do. We're not romantic. We are not sexy. We don't look like Bela Lugosi or Christopher Lee or Stephen Moyer. We don't behave like Dracula or Lestat or Edward Cullen.

We do not fucking sparkle.

Forget everything you've seen in movies and on television and video games, and everything you've read in books and comics. The vast majority of that stuff is bullshit.

Like I said earlier, vampires are more like sharks than they are human beings.

I slept that entire first day, until the sun had gone down again. When I finally woke up, it was with a hunger unlike anything I had ever felt before. I mean, it was downright painful how famished I was. When I woke up, I stumbled through the dark house and into the kitchen, where I found a note from Alicia, saying that she'd gone out to get a pizza and would be home shortly, and she hoped I was feeling better because I'd been asleep all day.

My stomach did flip-flops at the thought of pizza. I absentmindedly opened the cupboard and stared at all the mason jars full of canned goods from our garden, and the bags of chips and pretzels and trail mix, and then I threw up all over the floor. But what I vomited wasn't puke or even bile. It was a noxious black fluid.

A kind I'd seen before.

I sat down on the floor, and pulled my pajama pants up over my ankle, and was surprised to see that my wounds had healed. All that was left was some faint scarring, and I reckoned that would fade, as well, just as soon as I ate.

It wasn't Donny's nails that had torn at me. It was his teeth. And unlike him, it hadn't taken a few minutes to turn me into one of them. It had taken all day. At some point between the time I'd gotten home and now, I had died in there on my bed. Died in my sleep.

And woke up as this.

I said that vampires don't feel love or angst, at least, not the way that humans do. And that's true. But we do feel something akin to them. That's what stopped me at the last minute from completely draining Alicia, the way Donny had done to Darnell. It took all of my willpower, and all of my self-control, but at the last moment, I was able to tear myself away from my daughter, so that she became like me, rather than just an empty husk.

We talked about it some the next night, and then we went out hunting together. We brought down two deer, and shared them. We would have probably done the same thing to a human being, if one of y'all had crossed our paths first, but it was after dark, and the roads were empty, and so it was two deer instead. That was a nice time, hunting together like that, sharing the thrill of the chase, and the excitement of the kill, and gorging ourselves happily until those deer were exsanguinated and we were so full our bellies were swollen. It was something we could do together—a father and daughter bonding activity, just like when we used to have movie nights and puzzle nights and all the other things we've done together over the years since her mom died. We'd both been afraid of those times coming to an end, once Alicia had headed off for college. But now we didn't have to be afraid of them any longer. There's no reason for her to go to Morgantown anymore, and even if there was, it's probably not a good idea for a vampire to attend college—at least not until we both have a better handle on everything, and a better understanding of what we can and cannot do, and what will kill us. Donny was right about the innate knowledge that comes with the transformation, but I'm inclined to be cautious about things. You may think I'm being overprotective, but if so, I don't care. Alicia is still my daughter. That hasn't changed. The only thing that has changed is what we are.

And it's not like we're going to age. That's another part the books and movies got right. Vampires don't age. We can decline, if we don't eat. We can fade, like those poor bastards in the cave. But we don't age.

It's been four days for me. Three for Alicia. The police have been here twice, maybe looking to interview me, or maybe just looking for me in general. We managed to hide from them each time, but the pull—the desire to feed—was hard to suppress, especially for Alicia. If they come back again, I don't think either one of us will be able to help ourselves.

They must have found Terry's truck by now, and I would reckon they've probably explored the farm, and the surrounding fields and hills and forests. Which means that they've probably searched the hollow, as well. But probably during daylight, and I'm guessing they didn't find anything. And that they got out of there before sundown. I wonder how it was for Donny, huddled below ground with a bunch of strangers, hiding and hungry while those humans tromped around above?

I also wonder about Gray, and the chance that maybe he didn't die. That maybe he's like me and Donny and Alicia are now. After all, I didn't see him die, the way I did Seymour and Cecil and Mattie and

Terry. I didn't see what was left of his corpse the way I did Darnell's. All I know for sure is that the vampire sucked his eyeball out. Is there a chance he could be in the cave with them? Probably not.

But it's worth checking out, regardless.

Back in the hollow, when Donny first changed, he could sense the other vampires. He could hear and see them in his thoughts. I haven't been able to do that. I can do it with Alicia, but not the others. My guess is that we're too far away from there, but I don't know for sure. I'm still new to this, remember. And that's another reason why I need to return back to that place.

I hope that Gray is a vampire, if only so I can apologize to him, and tell him how sorry I am about being angry about the meth thing. I'm just as guilty as anyone. After all, it was me who suggested we go check the hollow out. And in truth, while Gray's plan to make meth may have been harebrained, it led to something pretty wonderful. I'm grateful to him for that, and I'd like him to know it. So, I'm going to go look for him. And if he's not there—if he's not a vampire—then it's even more important to return to the hollow.

Because of Donny.

I keep remembering what Donny said, when we were debating whether to press deeper into the hollow.

"I ain't got no family except y'all," Donny said. *"I'll come, too."*

Donny shouldn't be left alone there.

He should be with family.

He should be with us.

Alicia and I have been experimenting with minced garlic from the refrigerator. We've been seeing just how close we can get to it before it begins to affect us. Seems to be about eight feet. The reach on Terry's backhoe is twelve feet. So, what I'm going to do tonight, after the sun goes down, is pay a visit to Terry's wife and kids. I'm going to let them know that everything is going to be okay, and after Alicia and I have fed on them a little bit, I'll leave her there at the house to watch over them while they change. Meanwhile, I'm going to get the backhoe out of Terry's barn, and take it down to the edge of that hollow, and clear out some of that fucking wild garlic.

And then I'll see Donny again.

And maybe Gray.

That's one thing we vampires have, that you don't ever see reflected in the books and movies.

We have hope.

END

AFTERWORD: THE DEVIL'S DETAILS

ANYBODY WHO HAS read more than two books or stories written by me realizes fairly quickly that all of my works take place in the same shared literary universe. Everything from the very first short story I ever published to this novella which you just finished reading? They're all connected. For the most part, I keep that interconnective tissue subtle. I don't want the continuity to be a burden to readers. You shouldn't have to be familiar with one book to understand and enjoy a different book. Each reader discovers me through a different novel or story, so each novel and story has to be written with accessibility in mind.

Of course, these days, the idea of interconnected media properties and shared universes are nothing new. The big screen success of the Marvel Universe and other such franchises have embedded an understanding of the concept of the shared universe in the minds of just about every consumer in the world, regardless of their familiarity with genre or geek culture. But when I was a kid, such a thing was unheard of. Sure, big comic book geek that I was in the 1970s and 1980s, I understood that all of Marvel and DC's stories were taking place in their own shared universes. I understood that a plot point in this month's issue of *The Defenders* of *Doctor Strange* might impact a future issue of *The Amazing Spider-Man* or *Ka-Zar* or *Iron Man*. But—hard as it might be for my Millennial and Generation Z readers to believe—most people around me did not know that. The concept was unfathomable to them. I suspect that's why Stephen King's stuff got an extra boost of fan power in the early 1980s. General readers began to figure out that all f it was taking place in a shared universe. The publication of *The Dark Tower* series fully solidified that.

Obviously, the trifecta of the Marvel Comics universe, the DC Comics universe, and the Stephen King universe had a huge impact on me as a reader, and later on as a developing writer. I knew from Day One that I wanted all of my stuff to take place in a shared universe. And over the last twenty-five years, I've built that universe up, brick by brick.

WITH TEETH was a brick that I left on the kiln for a very long time. I've had both the idea and the title bouncing around in my head since the mid-2000's. Indeed, I pitched it t Leisure Books back around 2008 or 2009. Sadly, I was never able to interest a publisher in the idea, and thus, I put it on the back-burner—finally writing it between December 2020 and January 2021. But alert readers will notice that I laid the bricks for it long before that.

Following this Afterword are two other vampire stories that I've written during my career. The first, "Down Under" was written in 1995 and first published in 1997. The second, "The Last Supper" was written and published in 2015. That's five years before I wrote **WITH TEETH** and yet—within that short story— you'll find a reference to the clan of West Virginia vampires you just read about, as well as a reference to the vampires from the earlier short story.

So, with that, let's get to "Down Under" and "The Last Supper"!

Enjoy . . .

—Brian Keene, somewhere along the Susquehanna River, March 2021

THE LAST SUPPER

A FEW MINUTES before he heard the sound, Carter became convinced that the trees were following him.

He'd been walking from the Edgefield Hotel toward the town of Troutdale, just past the point where Halsey Street turned into Historic Highway 30. The moon shone overhead, three-quarters full in a cloudless sky, providing enough light to see—not that he needed the illumination. Carter saw clearly even on the darkest of nights, and his hearing and sense of smell were equally hyper-attuned.

A vast mountain range spanned the horizon to his left. He thought that the peaks might be related to Mount Hood, but he couldn't be sure, and there was no one to ask. Nor could he pull out his phone and find out via the Internet, because both had stopped working months ago. He walked on, once again certain that the trees were following him. He heard them behind him, shuffling forward, tiptoeing on their roots. Every time he stopped and turned to glare at them, the trees stopped, too.

"I'm crazy."

His voice sounded funny to him, and his throat

was sore. How long had it been since he'd spoken aloud? He couldn't remember.

"I'm crazy," he repeated. "That's all. And I'd have to be, wouldn't I? Living alone like this? It's enough to drive anyone crazy."

He walked on, trying his best to ignore the trees. To his right was a field lined with rows of grapes. The unattended crop had grown wild. Vines, heavy with fruit, sprawled out into the road and snaked up trees and telephone poles.

The rustling sounds started again. He was sure they were real this time. He spun around.

"Stop following me!"

The trees didn't answer.

Carter turned, stumbled over a pothole in the road, and winced as a jolt of pain ran through his leg. He'd broken it two weeks before, which was why he'd holed up at Edgefield Hotel for so long. Before the epidemic, such an injury would have healed more quickly, but food had been in scarce supply, and thus, it had taken longer. Before the Edgefield, he'd last eaten in Seattle, and that had only been a starving, rail-thin feral dog—barely enough blood to sustain him and certainly lacking in the vitamins and nutrients he needed to effectively heal.

He'd spent a few days in Seattle, scrounging, before ultimately moving on, but the dog had been his only encounter. Seattle, like everywhere else in the world, had been emptied by the plague, its population reduced to nothing but bags of rotten meat filled with congealed, sludge-like blood. The stench wafting out of the city had been noticeable from miles away, and Carter had been certain that it would have been even to someone without his heightened sense of smell.

Unfortunately, there had been no one else left to smell it.

He'd made his way on foot from Seattle down into Oregon. Driving had been out of the question. The roads were choked with abandoned cars, wreckage, downed trees, and bodies. They'd cleared a bit in Oregon, but he'd continued walking anyway, because it made it easier to hunt. He'd reached Troutdale, and broke into the Edgefield, intent on sleeping through the day and then continuing on toward Portland that night, when a stray beam of sunlight had altered those plans. He'd been climbing a stairwell, listening to his footfalls echo through the deserted building, sniffing around and sifting through the thick miasma of dust, mildew, long-spoiled food, even longer-spoiled corpses, when the first light of the rising sun had drifted through a window and struck him on the arm. Flinching, Carter had recoiled. The next thing he knew, he'd lost his balance and tumbled down the stairs. He heard his leg break before the pain set in. Then, he'd lost consciousness.

When he awoke, daylight had begun to stream through the empty halls. Panicked, Carter crawled into an alcove behind the stairwell and huddled in the darkness, shivering with agony and shock. He'd remained there until nightfall, when at last, feverish and half-delirious with pain, he crawled out again and managed to find a hotel room with a door ajar. He'd dragged himself inside and shut the door. With great difficulty, he'd managed to drape a moldy bedspread over the room's lone window before collapsing with exhaustion. Then he'd slept.

On his second night in the Edgefield, he'd heard a faint skittering from out in the hall. Alert, he'd sat up in bed, sniffing the air. Slowly, he crawled to the door and opened it. Then he lay there, still as death. He waited a full hour before the rat investigated, and it took another twenty minutes of motionlessness before the animal was brave enough to come close to him and take an experimental nibble, at which point Carter reached out and grabbed it, seizing the creature with both hands. After he'd eaten, he rested again, allowing his leg to heal.

And now, here he was, intent upon exploring Troutdale before sunrise. If his efforts were unsuccessful, he'd move on to Portland tomorrow night. He doubted that Portland would offer anything more than Seattle had, but it was something to do. And, in truth, it wasn't just food he was looking for. It was companionship.

Carter was lonely.

The irony wasn't lost on him. He was, as far as he knew, the last living human on the planet, except that he wasn't alive and he wasn't human. He hadn't been either for a long time.

The breeze shifted and Carter caught a whiff of the grapes. It had been decades since he'd tasted grapes— or jelly or wine or anything else made from them. Decades since he'd tasted food of any sort—pasta, beef, ice cream, vegetables. Chocolate.

Carter sighed. He'd loved chocolate as a boy. Sometimes, he tried to remember what it had really tasted like, but the memory was fleeting. A ghost—a gossamer phantasm as insubstantial and romanticized as the memory of a first kiss. Over the years, he'd grown accustomed to being a vampire, but Carter had never quite gotten used to not being able to have chocolate. He'd tried several times—once right after his transformation, and a few times since. On each occasion, the chocolate had acted as a toxin in his system. All foods had the same effect. He wasn't lactose or gluten intolerant. He suffered from a food allergy, and it encompassed all foods. All except blood.

Carter died on June 17, 1967, at the Monterey Pop Festival, during the beginning of the Summer of Love. A still mostly unknown Jimi Hendrix had just begun the opening chords of "Wild Thing" when Carter, high as a kite and feeling happy, had gone outside the fairgrounds hand-in-hand with a beautiful brunette who had never given him her name but had looked a little bit like Grace Slick. They'd begun to make love in a dark area behind a porta-potty, except that the love turned to terror very quickly, as the girl's soft, eager kisses on his throat had turned frenzied, and then sharp. And then . . .

. . . nothing.

He'd been lost in a dream haze, not unlike an acid trip. To this day his memories were sketchy at best. Someone, perhaps a fellow concertgoer or one of the outnumbered security guards, had interrupted them. They must have, because she'd never had the opportunity to drink him dry. If she had, he wouldn't be here today. Carter had a vague memory of being loaded into an ambulance, and another of a paramedic leaning over him, aghast, and muttering, "Jesus, look at his fucking throat! It's like a wild animal got at him or something." Then, much later, he'd regained consciousness inside a morgue. His first thought, upon waking, was that he'd missed the rest of Hendrix's set, but had certainly experienced his very own wild thing.

Carter had figured out fairly quickly what he was. That was the easy part. Discovering which portions of the vampire legends were true, and which were bullshit, had taken a little longer. He was vulnerable to sunlight and garlic, but things like crosses and other religious trappings had no effect on him. He saw himself in the mirror just fine, albeit his reflection didn't age the way others did. He was perpetually twenty-two. He didn't know if a stake through the heart could kill him or not, but gunshots, a stabbing, and being hit by a tractor-trailer one time in the Eighties hadn't. He'd recovered from those injuries as easily as he'd re-knit his broken leg. He'd also recovered from a spinal fracture suffered shortly after his transformation, when he'd jumped off a building in an attempt to turn into a bat. That last part of the vampire legend, as it turned out, was also just myth, as were the supposed abilities to control animals such as rats or influence and hypnotize people.

He'd never again seen the vampire who'd turned him. Indeed, in the years that followed, Carter had only known two others like him. One had been a girl he himself had turned in the early-Seventies—a red-headed flower-child named Lindsey. They'd met at a Grateful Dead concert, and Carter had fallen in love almost immediately. For months, he kept his secret from her, until one night, when Lindsey was high and fantasizing out loud about what a cool trip it would be to live forever, and Carter had told her that he could make that possible.

And then he had.

Lindsey hadn't accepted it well, and a few days later, when the hunger for blood had become overwhelming, she'd opted to commit suicide by watching the sunrise, rather than feeding on another human. Sometimes, when he slept, Carter still smelled her burning, and heard her accusatory screams.

The other one like him had been Nick, a witty, fast-talking Greek who claimed to be over two hundred years old. Nick also claimed that he had helped to invent socialism. They'd met in Berkeley in 1986. Carter had been feeding in an alley behind a bookstore, after attending a poetry reading. When he'd finished, he'd become aware of the other vampire's presence. Nick had stood watching, a bemused expression on his face. Carter had been astonished to meet another like himself, and Nick became a mentor of sorts. He'd told Carter their kind were few and far between. Pop-culture depictions of vampire hierarchies and councils were bullshit. The only community Nick had known about was in the backwoods of West Virginia, and they were foul, savage creatures, more akin to a feral dog pack than civilized beings such as Carter and himself.

Nick had gone to North Korea shortly after Bush succeeded Reagan. Carter hadn't heard from him since. He often wondered what had happened to his friend, especially since the plague.

He was so lonely.

Nick had sometimes teased Carter about his friendships with humans, asking him if the butcher made friends with the cows before he slaughtered them.

Carter thought of that now, as Troutdale grew closer. And yes, he thought, yes the butcher would befriend the cows, because he'd be so happy just to have someone to talk to again.

He walked into town, passing under a wrought iron arch with two fish statues on either side. A sign proclaimed WELCOME TO TROUTDALE—THE WESTERN GATEWAY. A gateway to what, Carter wondered? Another world? How wonderful would that be, to slip from one dimension to the next, and travel to a reality where the plague had never happened and he wasn't starving and there were people to talk to and laugh with. If only it were that easy.

Carter passed an outlet mall. Most of the storefront windows were broken, and a tree had fallen through the roof of the bookstore, allowing the elements to get inside. He paused for a moment, listening and sniffing the air, but as far as he could tell, the mall was deserted. If he got closer, it might be possible to discern a rat or squirrel living among the ruins, but that would have involved an arduous climb down a steep embankment. Carter instead decided to try his luck deeper into town.

The main drag was lined with small shops—a tattoo parlor, several attorney's offices, a chiropractor, a dentist, a hair salon, and a spa were mixed in amongst numerous bars and restaurants. All of them were deserted, their occupants long gone. He paused in front of an antiques store. A faded, yellowed newspaper cartoon had been taped inside the window. Its edges were brown and curling. In it, a young boy and his pet tiger were snuggled together in bed. The caption read, *Things are never quite as scary when you've got a best friend.* Carter supposed this was true, because he was fucking terrified. His nights were spent in constant fear. Mostly, he was scared of being alone.

The other side of Troutdale butted up against the Sandy River. There, in a wooded area behind the Depot Rail Museum, he found the remains of a homeless encampment. A blue plastic tarp had been stretched out between four tree trunks, and tied fast, forming a makeshift roof. Beneath it was a stone fire pit, filled with charred sticks. Judging by the mud inside the circle of rocks, it had been quite some time since a fire had burned there.

"Hello," he called. Rather than echoing, his voice seemed to fall flat, as if the forest itself had swallowed it. It faded all too quickly, replaced again by silence. Carter longed for the drone of an airplane overhead, or the rumbling of a train or a bus passing by, but there was nothing. Even the birds and animals had gone silent, no doubt as a result of his presence.

Sighing, Carter turned back to town, intent on finding something to eat. Out of the corner of his eye, the trees seemed to turn with him. He wheeled to face them.

"I told you to stop following me! Leave me alone."

And that was when he heard the sound. It started as a distant whoosh of air, with a low, mechanical hum beneath it. He recognized the noise right away. It was the faraway sound of a car on the highway, coming closer. Carter glanced around frantically, trying to determine its origin. Then, as it drew nearer, he ran back down the street. While flying or transforming into a bat might have been the stuff of fanciful legend, Carter was indeed equipped with unnatural speed and strength, both of which he relied upon now, dashing the entire length of Troutdale in just under thirty seconds. But the exertion left him winded, and he was still weak from hunger, and he had to stop again beneath the fish archway, panting.

He had to be imagining it. Deep down inside, he knew this to be true. There couldn't be a car. It was a mirage. A hallucination. Just like the trees.

But what if it wasn't?

The hum of the engine and tires grew ever closer. He limped quickly to the overpass and gazed out at the highway below. There, on the horizon, he saw headlights. It was real! Carter had no idea how the driver had managed to wrangle around the assorted wreckage choking the highways, but at that moment, he didn't care. His pulse hammered in his throat as the car drew nearer. Human beings! One, at the very least. His excitement gave way to panic. What if they were . . . bad? Carter had seen enough post-apocalyptic movies and read enough dystopian fiction that visions of leather-clad punk rock marauders filled his head. But, no. Given just how much of humanity had died off, the driver and any possible occupants couldn't be bad. He couldn't justify this assurance with any sound logic, but that didn't stop him from clinging to the emotion. They had to be decent, and surely they'd be grateful to see him, as well.

"Hello," Carter shouted from the overpass. "Up here!"

He realized they'd never see him from atop the

overpass. While the car wasn't speeding, it was nighttime, and the driver was probably focused on the road ahead, alert for any wreckage or obstructions in the dark. He hurried down the embankment, heading toward the road. The occupants of the car must be driving with the window down, he decided, because now he could smell them. The scent was faint, but undeniable. A woman, unless he was mistaken. Although he couldn't be sure, he suspected she was alone.

He slid down the hillside and dashed out into the roadway. Headlights speared him. Carter raised his arms over his head and waved them enthusiastically.

"Hello," he called. "Stop the car! Please stop."

Tires squealed as the driver locked the brakes. He smelled rubber burning, and caught a glimpse of the frightened woman's face through the windshield as the car swerved to one side and spun out of control. Then, as if in slow motion, the car flipped over and slid on its roof. Metal shrieked, and so did the driver. Sparks danced in the darkness like fireflies. There was a deafening crash as the upside-down vehicle slammed into the concrete support beneath the overpass, and then folded in on itself like aluminum foil.

Carter's heart beat once. Twice.

The driver had stopped screaming.

"No!" He ran toward the car, broken glass crunching beneath his feet. The stench of burnt rubber and scorched metal was thick in the air, but even thicker was the smell of blood. The odor simultaneously filled him with both excitement and dread, and Carter hated himself for feeling both.

He reached the wreck, got down on his hands and knees, and peered inside. Remarkably, the driver was conscious. She was pretty, African-American and in her mid-to-late twenties. Carter couldn't determine much else about her because she was covered in blood. The smell of it seemed to assail him, and he reeled back, weeping.

"Didn't . . . " Blood trickled from her mouth as she spoke. "You . . . surprised me."

"I'm sorry," he choked. "I'm so sorry. Are you okay?"

It was a stupid question, he knew. Judging by the lacerations on her body and the position of several limbs, the young woman was anything but okay. But after all that time spent talking to inanimate objects and himself, Carter was having trouble focusing on how to talk to another person. He took a deep breath, smelled the blood, and tried again, shivering as he did.

"My name is Carter. What's yours?"

"A . . . Ashley. Are you . . . really alive?"

He nodded, unable to form enough words to lie.

"It's . . . nice to . . . meet you, Carter. I . . . thought I was . . . "

"Alone," Carter finished for her, and smiled.

She returned the gesture and tried to nod. When she did, her expression changed to anguish.

Carter's choked laughter changed to a sob. "Don't try to move. Just stay still. You're going to be okay."

"I'm cold," she whispered. "Will you . . . stay with me?"

It was Carter's turn to nod. "Of course I will. I wouldn't leave you for anything. It's just . . . I just . . . I thought I'd never talk to anyone ever again."

"Me, too." More blood trickled from Ashley's mouth.

"I thought you were like the trees."

Ashley frowned in confusion. "W-what?"

"Never mind. It's not important."

Carter studied the wreckage. He could free her easily enough. A fire and rescue team's Jaws of Life had nothing on him, but if he did, she'd probably die within seconds. Mashed and mangled as she was, the twisted steel pressed so tightly against her was the only thing still keeping Ashley alive. Despite that, she probably only had minutes.

Carter began to cry.

"I'm sorry," he moaned. "I didn't mean to . . . "

"It's okay," Ashley reassured him. "Tell me . . . about yourself. Talk to me . . . until . . . "

So he did. As tears ran down his perpetually young cheeks, Carter spoke through muffled sobs. He shook with emotion while she trembled with shock. He held her hand, and it was soft and warm. They talked for a while, and then her hand turned cold, and she was gone.

Carter was still weeping as he began to feed.

DOWN UNDER

HE BOYS HAD disappeared over a week ago and as much as Kip hated to think about it, but the fact was, they were probably fish food. That was the whole point of this. Still, he had two kids of his own and dead children were the last thing he wanted in his head before the dive.

Kip adjusted his air tanks and glanced at his surroundings. The quarry had been off limits, posted against trespassers. Although he knew better, local legend said it was bottomless. Formerly used for mining iron ore, it was impossible to see more than a few feet into the depths of the black water. For decades, people had been dumping old tires, fence posts, barbed wire, refrigerators, televisions, and even cars into the quarry. Along with all that junk, the ruins of the old mining camp still stood at the bottom. Caution would be needed while swimming around in the muck.

A hand fell on his shoulder, and Kip jumped. Otto and the rest of the team laughed behind him.

"What's the matter, Kip? You're not getting jumpy are you?"

"Real funny, boss," Kip replied. "You've got to admit though, this place is creepy."

"So is my mother-in-law." Otto laughed. "I believe the stories about this place as much as I believe in the tooth fairy."

The other four divers chuckled, and Kip glared at them. Childs, a hulking, good humored black man, who Kip shot darts with every Friday night down at The Boar's Head. Pat, a short, shifty eyed man who was known for his love of liquor and his even greater love of any female other than his wife. Joe, who had been Kip's best man at his wedding ten years ago. Finally, there was Roger, who was joining the team from the state police underwater recovery division. In addition to the divers, there was Otto, who would stay up top and monitor their progress in case of emergencies, and Sheriff Laughman, who had led the fruitless search for the missing boys and had aged noticeably in the past month.

"I've got to agree with Kip," Roger said. "This place does feel spooky. What's the deal?"

"It's your town, Bob." Otto turned to the sheriff. "Why don't you tell him?"

"There's an old wife's tale about the quarry." The tired lawman loaded a pinch of Copenhagen into his mouth, spat once in the dirt, and continued. "Back around the early nineteen hundreds, most of this area was still forest. The only folks who lived around here were the miners and their families. They had a little shantytown built right down there in the center of the quarry—a camp, really. Mining for iron ore was a hard but honest living back then, and things were really starting to prosper for them."

He paused and spit again. The shore was silent, as if nature were engrossed in the tale.

"Supposedly, people started vanishing. It was mostly children at first, then the women, and finally the men. Supposedly, they didn't stay gone long, though. They came back."

"What do you mean?" Roger asked.

"Evil things, man," Childs answered. "They say the place was infested with the undead."

Roger laughed. "You guys had me going there for a minute. Pick on the State Trooper, huh? The undead!"

"Yeah," Otto said, "they've been feeding me that shit for years, too. Ever since I first moved here."

Joe shook his head. "Laugh if you want, Otto, but there's more to it."

From the center of the quarry came a loud splash, causing them all to jump.

"I don't think we need to hear the rest," Pat said, glancing out at the water.

Kip followed his gaze. Rings were spreading from the center to gently lap at the shoreline.

The sheriff cleared his throat and continued anyway. "This much is a historical fact. One of the men from the camp took the dynamite they used for mining and blew up the dam. The river flooded this entire valley. When the water settled, this lake formed right over top of the mines and the camp. The fellow who did it was the only survivor. When the authorities caught him, he was clearly insane. He claimed the running water was the only means to kill what lived there."

"Enough," Otto said. "It's time to go to work. Later on, we'll build a campfire and you girls can tell all the stories you want."

Roger looked visibly shaken. He fumbled with his mouthpiece and air tanks while the others walked down to the shore.

"Come on, Lieutenant." Kip put a hand around his shoulder. "Otto may be an asshole, but he's right. It's just a story."

They lined up and tested their equipment, while Otto ran through a last-minute checklist.

"Now remember, space yourselves out down there. We've got a lot of area to cover. If the kids are down under, their bodies are probably caught in something. Be careful that the same thing doesn't happen to you. The water's full of crap. It's dark, and even with your floodlights on, visibility will be poor. Watch each other's backs. If you find the kids, release your packet of red dye to mark where the bodies are located."

The sheriff saluted. "Good luck, fellas. Be careful."

They walked into the water. Childs and Roger went first, with Pat in the middle, and Kip and Joe bringing up the rear.

Otto and the Sheriff watched until their heads sank below the surface. Hand trembling, Sheriff Laughman fumbled out his tobacco can.

"What's wrong, Bob?"

"Just thinking about something," the lawman replied. "Every year, the Game Association stocks this with fish, but it's not heavily fished by anyone."

"What's your point?"

"My point is, what happens to all those fish?"

They fell silent. Overhead, an unseen whippoorwill sang its lonely song.

They waited.

Kip felt a moment of panic as the ebony water closed over his head. He fought it off and followed along in formation. The lake *was* deep and did indeed seem bottomless. There was no gradual sloping of the shore, just an immediate twenty-foot drop off.

They proceeded farther into the murky depths. Childs gave a hand signal and they switched on their lights. The watery depths were a maze of tires, bedsprings, refrigerators and other miscellaneous junk. An enormous catfish swam lazily by them, its body covered with dangling, blood engorged leeches. A queasy shiver ran through Kip as he watched. He hoped to himself that they didn't encounter any snakes. Since childhood, Joe had been terrified of them. He'd run home screaming every time they'd come across one in their boyhood expeditions.

The rusted shell of a car lay belly up, minnows flitting through its innards. Moving slowly through the stagnant water, Joe and Kip approached it. The others fanned out and began to search the bottom of the quarry.

Curiously, Kip saw few fish, other than the leech-ridden catfish.

Pat motioned ahead, indicating the slime-covered bones of the mining town, still standing after decades in the submerged night. He, Childs and Roger swam off toward it, their floodlights cutting a swath through the gloom.

Kip and Joe approached the car, shining their lights through the shattered windshield.

Something stirred within.

With one glance at the serpentine forms wriggling inside, Joe turned, darting for the surface. Kip recoiled in disgust as the writhing ass of snakes uncoiled sluggishly from their nest to investigate the disturbance. Kip cautiously backed away.

He didn't notice the two shadows that detached themselves from the muddy bottom and swam after his friend.

Dodging the snakes, Kip swam toward the sunken buildings, joining the rest of the team. He could dimly make them out as they moved from structure to structure, shining their lights through the murk and silt. Childs gave him a puzzled look as he approached. Kip motioned upward and then pointed back to the snakes, which were slowly returning to the old car. The floodlights failed to penetrate the darkness beyond. Kip pointed toward the surface, trying to indicate that Joe had fled.

Childs shook his head.

They turned their attention back to the submerged ghost town.

Joe's head burst from the calm lake surface twenty yards from the shore. He gasped, spitting out his mouthpiece and glancing frantically about.

Otto jumped to his feet. "Did you find them?"

"Sn . . . snakes!"

Joe started to swim for the shore, but he paused.

"Quit fucking around and get back down there!"

"Something just brushed against my leg," Joe yelled. "Ouch! It bit me!"

From where they stood, Otto and the sheriff saw the shadowy outlines of two figures underwater, pulling on Joe's legs.

"What the hell?" Sheriff Laughman stood up.

"It's the other guys," Otto said. "They'll handle it."

Joe vanished, tugged back under.

Otto sat back down and relaxed. "Told you. They aren't putting up with his bullshit."

The sheriff shook his head. "Something doesn't feel right."

"What?"

"I don't know." He shrugged. "Something."

Under the surface of the lake, Joe gaped in terror at the figures clutching him. When he opened his mouth to scream, stagnant water rushed into his lungs. He was dead by the time they dragged him to the bottom. His open veins left a scarlet trail.

Five minutes after dying, Joe opened his eyes.

The divers grouped together outside the remains of an old barn. Its frame remained upright and fish darted from the hundreds of rotten holes that peppered its walls. Kip and Pat shined their lights in a wide arc as they approached the structure. Childs and Roger followed behind.

Kip's light fell across a still, white form. He took a deep breath from his air tank. They had found one of the boys.

Curiously, the corpse was not bloated. Perplexed, Kip and Pat moved closer while Roger stood motionless and Childs glanced uneasily about. Pat leaned over the inert form, reaching with outstretched fingers, and closed the kid's glassy eyes.

The eyes opened again.

The boy sat up quickly. His lips curled back, displaying gleaming white fangs. He reached for Pat with hands that had sprouted talon-like fingernails. Pat struggled as it grasped him behind the head. With inhuman strength, it pulled the helpless diver toward its greedy mouth. Latching onto Pat's throat, its teeth slashed through the wetsuit and sliced his flesh in an explosion of red.

Roger backed up in horror, bumping into another shadowy figure behind him. Dozens of pale arms encircled him. Wicked talons flayed open his torso. Childs struggled to his aid, flinging the ghostly forms through the water. Then, he too was covered in swarming bodies. He fought wildly as they dragged him along the quarry bottom toward the barn. His valiant thrashing stirred up a cloud of dark mud that encircled both hunters and prey. Kip watched in horror as a legion of fangs tore into Child's body. Then they were obscured from view.

With all his strength, Kip darted an attacking creature and swam for the surface. His thoughts were a chaotic jumble. The stories were true! How had the creatures survived the running water? Had they burrowed beneath the mines until the waters were still?

Throwing a terrified glance below him, he was relieved to see no pursuit. The swarm of creatures were busy with the others. A crimson cloud rose from the carnage, climbing slowly towards the surface.

He kicked for the top. From high above, he suddenly spied Joe swimming to his rescue. Kip firmly grasped Joe's outstretched hand. It dawned on him that his best friend wore no facemask. Pain lashed through his wrist. Talons had burst from Joe's fingertips.

Joe smiled, his fangs gleaming in the red water, and welcomed his friend down under.

Sheriff Laughman pointed at the water. "Something's happening, Otto."

A dark, red cloud had risen to the top of the lake and was slowly spreading through the water.

"That's a red dye pack," Otto said. "They've found the bodies."

Dusk turned to twilight and the shadows around them grew longer.

The sheriff radioed the county coroner. Then he turned back to Otto. "What do we do now?"

"We wait for them to come up."

They sat and waited, smoke from Otto's cigarette drifting off into the approaching night. The sheriff winced. His tobacco tasted sour in his suddenly dry mouth.

The sun disappeared behind the hills and darkness fell upon the shoreline.

The men surfaced and swam towards them.

ABOUT THE AUTHOR

BRIAN KEENE writes novels, comic books, short fiction, and occasional journalism for money. He is the author of over forty books, mostly in the horror, crime, and dark fantasy genres. Keene's 2003 novel, *The Rising*, is often credited (along with Robert Kirkman's *The Walking Dead* comic and Danny Boyle's *28 Days Later* film) with inspiring pop culture's current interest in zombies. Keene's works have been translated into German, Spanish, Russian, Polish, Italian, French, Taiwanese, and many more. In addition to his own original work, Keene has written for media properties such as *Doctor Who, The X-Files, Hellboy, Masters of the Universe, Alien*, and *Thor*.

Several of Keene's novels and stories have been adapted for film, including *Ghoul*, *The Naughty List*, *The Ties That Bind*, and *Fast Zombies Suck*. Several more are in-development or under option. Keene also served as Executive Producer for the feature length film *I'm Dreaming of a White Doomsday*.

Keene's work has been praised in such diverse places as *The New York Times, The History Channel, The Howard Stern Show, CNN, The Huffington Post, Publisher's Weekly, Media Bistro, Fangoria Magazine, Bloody Disgusting,* and *Rue Morgue Magazine.* He has won numerous awards and honors, including the 2014 World Horror Grandmaster Award, 2001 Bram Stoker Award for Nonfiction, 2003 Bram Stoker Award for First Novel, the 2016 Imadjinn Award for Best Fantasy Novel, the 2015 Imaginarium Film Festival Awards for Best Screenplay, Best Short Film Genre, and Best Short Film Overall, the 2004 Shocker Award for Book of the Year, and Honors from United States Army International Security Assistance Force in Afghanistan and Whiteman A.F.B. (home of the B-2 Stealth Bomber) 509th Logistics Fuels Flight. A prolific public speaker, Keene has delivered talks at conventions, college campuses, theaters, and inside Central Intelligence Agency headquarters in Langley, VA.

Keene serves on the Board of Directors for the Scares That Care 501c charity organization.

He lives in rural Pennsylvania with author Mary SanGiovanni.

For more information, visit BrianKeene.com

Made in United States
North Haven, CT
17 July 2022